"Damn it, Spence!
In our own house?"

"Sharley." Spence sounded as if something had hit him very hard just beneath the ribs. "Sharley, please." He put a hand out. "I can explain."

The woman on the love seat—*Sharley's* love seat— clutched at Spence's sleeve. There was panic on her face. "No, you can't, Spence."

He looked down at her and bit his lip.

"There seems to be a difference of opinion," Sharley said. "And though I hate to say it, I agree with your secretary on this one. I don't see how you can explain. But I'm listening. Why don't you try."

Spence was silent.

"Nothing at all to say?" Sharley's voice was almost gentle. "I guess I'm not surprised." Then she turned her back on him, walked to the door and shut it very firmly behind her.

Leigh Michaels has been a writer since she was old enough to figure out how to hold a pencil, but publishing a romance novel was an ambition she kept secret from everyone except her husband—her biggest supporter. They mailed her first manuscript together on Friday the 13th, which she says has been her lucky day ever since.

She finds writing to be like tiptoeing into a parallel universe that's always waiting just around the corner from real life. All the people from all her books—the forty she's already written and the dozens more still waiting to be put on paper—live there and sometimes interact in unexpected ways, making going to work every day a new adventure.

Leigh loves to hear from readers; you can write to her at P.O. Box 935, Ottumwa, Iowa, 52501-0935.

Books by Leigh Michaels

HARLEQUIN ROMANCE
3214—THE BEST-MADE PLANS
3233—THE UNEXPECTED LANDLORD
3248—SAFE IN MY HEART
3263—TIES THAT BLIND
3275—THE LAKE EFFECT
3290—DATING GAMES

A SINGULAR HONEYMOON
Leigh Michaels

Harlequin Books

TORONTO • NEW YORK • LONDON
AMSTERDAM • PARIS • SYDNEY • HAMBURG
STOCKHOLM • ATHENS • TOKYO • MILAN
MADRID • WARSAW • BUDAPEST • AUCKLAND

To Margaret—
with thanks for your research
and CO-operation!

ISBN 0-373-03300-1

A SINGULAR HONEYMOON

Copyright © 1994 by Leigh Michaels.

This edition published by arrangement with Harlequin Enterprises B. V.

® and TM are trademarks of the publisher. Trademarks indicated with
® are registered in the United States Patent and Trademark Office, the
Canadian Trade Marks Office and in other countries.

Printed in U.S.A.

CHAPTER ONE

A RUSTLE IN THE BACK of the room caught Sharley's attention, and she looked up from the paper she was grading. It was the middle of a Friday afternoon, with just ten minutes to go till recess, and it would be no surprise if her second-graders were getting restless. But twenty small heads were bent over a math quiz and—

No, Sharley corrected. Nineteen students were doing a math quiz; one was using the test sheet to make a paper airplane. She sighed and beckoned him to bring it to her desk at the front of the room. "If you've finished with the test, Josh," she pointed out, "you may, very quietly, take up another activity."

Josh gave her a gap-toothed grin, smoothed the folds out of his quiz and went over to the window near her desk. "Miss Collins, look at the pretty red bird," he said a moment later in a loud whisper.

Sharley glanced toward the feeder just outside the window. The children filled it every morning, and their efforts had been rewarded through the entire winter. Today, a bright scarlet bird preened his feathers between bites of birdseed.

"Do you remember what that bird is called?" she asked Josh.

He frowned and finally shook his head.

"It's a cardinal," Sharley said. "You can tell by the orange beak and the funny peak on its head. Now, can you remember if a red cardinal is a male or a female?"

Josh's frown cleared. "It's a girl," he declared, "'cuz girls always get to wear the best colors." He came back to her desk and patted the sleeve of her electric-blue sweater. "And they get the sparkliest stuff, too," he added, pointing at the full-carat diamond in the ring on her left hand. "I don't see why they should, though."

Sharley turned her hand so the diamond caught the light. It certainly sparkled, even under the flat fluorescent lights of the classroom, but it was not as brilliant as Spence's eyes had been the night he had slipped the ring on her finger.... This, she reminded herself, was no time for daydreaming. "Are you certain of your theory about colors, Josh? It isn't always true in the case of birds, at least. That's a male cardinal."

"Really? He's a boy? Hot dog!" His eyes brightened and he headed back to the window.

Sharley turned her attention to his quiz. He hadn't even missed the tricky questions. Well, that was another thing to add to her list of homework this weekend—think out half a dozen new ways to challenge Josh at math. That would get her through six more school days, if she was lucky.

The quizzes began to arrive at her desk in a flood, and the noise level in the room rose as students turned to other activities. By the time the recess bell rang, only two were still working over their papers, and Sharley had to prompt them to finish. She was a bit late herself in heading out to the playground to supervise, and she was still buttoning her coat as she pulled the classroom door shut behind her.

In the hallway, the other second-grade teacher paused and laughed. "That'll fix me," Amy Howell said cheerfully. "Trying to sneak something past you is worse than trying to fool my kids." She held out a box. It was about a foot square and two inches thick, brightly wrapped in foil paper with an enormous white bow on top.

Sharley looked at it doubtfully. From the way Amy was handling the box, it obviously weighed almost nothing. "What's the occasion?"

Amy groaned. "The girl's getting married in just over a week and she says what's the occasion! I couldn't exactly give you this at your shower here yesterday, because the principal would have had a heart attack."

Sharley's eyebrows arched delicately. "Then I suppose I shouldn't open it in front of the students, either."

"Or your Aunt Charlotte," Amy murmured. "She doesn't strike me as the type who would appreciate this sort of gift. But I'll bet Spence is. I'll leave it on your desk."

Sharley laughed and pushed open the heavy glass door that led to the playground. Everything looked and sounded normal; childish shrieks came from the tetherball pole and the group of girls skipping rope. Off in a corner, several girls were slowly marching up and down in a row. Each one of them had her hands clasped together in an almost prayerful attitude. Each held her head tilted just so. And each small foot was lifted high, then set down with precision on the asphalt.

Playing wedding, Sharley deduced. It had been a popular game around this particular playground for more than two months—since just after Christmas vacation, in fact, when Sharley had told her students in their sharing time that after March break she would no longer be Miss Collins, but Mrs. Greenfield.

Two months! Such a terribly short time to accomplish everything, and yet now that her wedding day was almost here it hardly seemed possible that so many weeks had flown by. Just eight more days and she would put on that elaborate satin-and-lace gown—the most beautiful gown in the world, her female students had declared yesterday as they begged her to describe it one more time—and walk down the aisle to the altar where Spence Greenfield waited.

Spence—wonderful, handsome, brilliant Spence, who could discuss anything from nuclear physics to the theory of relativity to how the world economy really worked. But he had chosen to spend his life with a woman whose definition of science was teaching Josh the difference between a cardinal and a woodpecker, and who counted the day a success if one more student learned to make correct change for a dollar.

Not that there was anything menial about her job. Second grade laid the foundations for a child's whole attitude toward learning and life, and if that wasn't important, Sharley didn't know what was. Besides, she loved being around kids, where the unexpected was the rule of the day.

And there was nothing wrong with her brain, either—even though Amy Howell had a point when she announced that sometimes after a long day with twenty seven-year-olds she felt as if there was spaghetti between her ears.

Still, Spence could have married anyone at all. And right up until Christmas, Sharley hadn't been so sure he wouldn't. It wasn't that he'd been dating anyone else steadily, but he certainly hadn't seemed to be paying much attention to her, either. He had come to dinner now and then, when her aunt Charlotte had invited him. But that didn't necessarily mean he wanted to see Sharley; it could have been simply because her uncle Martin was his boss. And though they had always found plenty of things to talk about on those evenings, it hadn't been anything personal—just politics and books and community affairs.

Of course, all that had been before the company Christmas party....

A small hand tugged at her sleeve and an anxious little girl asked, "Didn't you hear the bell, Miss Collins?"

The children were already lined up at the entrance, waiting for her to lead them in. Sharley shook her head at her own preoccupation.

It was a good thing they had decided on an early wedding, even if it *had* caused calamity with her schedule all spring. Fitting a wedding and a honeymoon into a brief spring break wasn't easy, but it was worth the effort. Next Thursday was the last day of school before the vacation began. On Friday she'd do her last-minute shopping, have lunch with her bridesmaids and fit in a massage and a manicure. The wedding was Saturday, and then she'd have a whole week alone with Spence in Nassau, at a resort where Aunt Charlotte had assured her they needn't see anyone but the room-service waiter unless they wanted.

A whole week, with nothing and no one to interrupt. It would be heaven....

Darn it, she thought. In order to have a whole week in Nassau, she was extending her spring break. And since she wouldn't be back when school took up session once more, she had to leave a couple of days' worth of lesson plans for the teacher filling in for her. How had she managed to let that slip her mind so completely?

Easily. There hadn't been room in her head for anything but Spence since Christmas.

After the final bell, Sharley settled down at her desk once more and began mapping out a strategy to keep a whole classroom full of inquisitive heads—and fingers— occupied for two full days.

Amy Howell looked in half an hour later. "Are you still hitting the books?"

Sharley pulled off her reading glasses and rubbed the bridge of her nose. "Come on in, Amy. Do you think my substitute can handle a spelling bee?"

"Depends on who it is." Amy folded herself into a small chair in the front row and stared at the brightly wrapped box on the corner of Sharley's desk. "Haven't you opened that package yet?"

"I was afraid to, in case the president of the PTA happened to stop in."

"I'll stand guard. Come on, I'm dying to see your reaction."

"That's the other reason I haven't opened it," Sharley admitted. But she slid the blade of her scissors under the tape and pulled the foil paper loose. Stamped atop the black box inside was the logo of the House of Dreams. "A nightie?" she speculated. "Honestly, Amy." She lifted the top off the box. Inside, nestled in yards of bright red tissue paper, was the sheerest and shortest black lace negligee Sharley had ever seen.

"Well?" Amy picked the garment up by its two tiny spaghetti straps. "What do you think Spence will say when you come out of the bathroom wearing this on your wedding night? Or perhaps more to the point, what do you think he'll do?" She giggled. "Honestly, Sharley, you're turning beet red."

"It's the reflection of the tissue paper."

"No, it's not. Come on, honey, you're going to marry the man. Don't be a prude."

That wasn't the case at all, Sharley thought. The fact that a woman was willing to wait for her wedding night didn't mean she was a prude. And it didn't mean she had an easy time of controlling her impulses, either. Sharley had no reason to worry about a lack of desire; there had been several times in the past two months when it would have been very easy to throw common sense to the winds.... But of course Spence understood why this was so important to her.

He might not exactly *appreciate* her feelings, Sharley thought with a glint of laughter, but he *understood*.

In any case, she wasn't about to try explaining her reasoning to Amy, who would probably hoot rudely at the idea that a woman who had been engaged for two months hadn't yet slept with her fiancé.

Amy seemed to have taken the silence for what it was— all the answer she was going to get. She took the scrap of black lace from Sharley's fingers and dropped it back into the box. "You'll have to let me know if it lives up to its name," she said. "It's called a ring negligee, because it's so delicate you're supposed to be able to pull it through a man's wedding ring." She frowned a little. "Though, come to think of it, if a man *has* a wedding ring ..."

"He ought to be wearing it, instead of experimenting with the lingerie, don't you think?" Sharley wondered if the stunt would work. She suspected it would; the lace was extremely fine and sheer. Besides, she'd playfully tried on Spence's wedding band the day she bought it. It was wide and heavy, and twice as big around as her own delicate engagement ring. She folded the lacy garment neatly into the box. "Thanks, dear. I'll tell you—within reason— about the reaction."

Amy grinned. "I hope for your sake I'm not disappointed." She reached for the small framed snapshot on the corner of Sharley's desk and held it at arm's length. "He's one extremely good-looking man," she mused. "I always was a soft touch for a guy with a dimple in his chin." She put the frame back on the desk.

Spence's warm smile gave such a tug to Sharley's heart she couldn't help smiling back. Amy was right; he was a handsome man, with dark hair and classic features. The cleft in that strong chin was an unexpected note, of course, but Sharley, too, had a soft spot for masculine dimples. At least, she thought, for that particular one.

But it wasn't good looks and dimples she'd fallen in love with, but things like the twinkle in his gray eyes, which was so strong, even in a photo, that it demanded a response. He'd been particularly mischievous the day she'd taken that picture, she recalled. She had stopped by Hudson Products on an unseasonably warm January day with a picnic basket and an invitation to a stolen lunch hour. Spence had come out of his office and leaned against his secretary's desk, his arms folded across the front of a very nice gray cashmere sweater, and Sharley had snatched her camera from the basket—

"Doesn't she bother you?" Amy asked. "Spence's secretary, I mean."

Sharley glanced at an out-of-focus figure at the edge of the photograph. "Wendy? Of course not."

"She's so attractive."

"In case you haven't noticed, darling," Sharley said in her most sultry voice, "so am I." She let her fingers trail through her golden blond hair in a sensuous gesture, and batted her eyelashes for good measure.

Amy laughed. "Especially in black lace, I'll bet. What are you doing this weekend? Resting up for the wedding?"

"No such luck, I'm afraid. I have lists of things still to do. And Aunt Charlotte was supposed to help serve desserts at the scholarship fund-raiser Saturday, but—"

"But she's feeling poorly, so you get to do it for her? Honestly, Sharley, she's always passing the things she doesn't want to do on to you, on the grounds that she doesn't feel well enough."

"Quite often she doesn't. After that stroke she had a few years ago, it's a wonder she feels up to doing anything at all. Besides, she and Uncle Martin do so much for me that standing in for Charlotte and cutting a cheesecake now and then is nothing."

"I suppose that's true," Amy murmured. "She could have given up altogether." She pulled herself up out of the tiny chair with a groan and said, "I'd better finish my lesson plans, too. And guess what I'm going to do all weekend."

"I'm afraid to," Sharley said frankly. She put her glasses back on and opened a textbook.

"I'm going to think very hard about what to give you and Spence for a housewarming gift."

Sharley wadded up a subtraction work sheet and threw it at her. Amy ducked and headed for the door, grinning.

THE MARCH AIR WAS deceptively mild for northern Iowa and the breeze held the first false promise of spring, as Sharley walked home that afternoon. Her long wool coat was far too heavy; she'd have taken it off, except that she didn't want to carry it. If this sort of warmth kept up over the weekend, a full-fledged epidemic of spring fever would race through the school, and next week, before the break began, would seem very long indeed.

Sharley saw several of her students along the way. Living in the neighborhood and walking back and forth was rather like being a cop on the beat, she thought sometimes. For one thing, it reminded her that her students were simply kids. For another, she often noticed something before it became a problem at school. Like cliques and sibling rivalries, for instance, or the moving van parked outside the Hollisters' house. Did that mean Amber Hollister's mother was carrying out her longtime threat to leave her husband and kids and go back to the East Coast? Sharley made a mental note to check on that first thing Monday morning. Amber had been awfully subdued today....

Sharley turned the corner into what Amy referred to as "the mansion district." In the first few blocks between the midtown school and her home, there were ranch houses, Colonials, bungalows. Most were neat and well kept, and all were on good-sized lots. But none of them could compete with the executive houses that lay along winding streets and cul-de-sacs a little farther from the center of town. Some of those homes were legitimate mansions.

Charlotte and Martin Hudson's house was one of them. It was deceptively simple from the outside—only one story and set well back from the street at an angle on a block-square lot. From the street, in fact, a passerby who peeked through the tall fence could see little more of the house than a low mass of pale gray brick, with bay windows and dark burgundy trim. And because of the trees and shrubs and bushes, it was impossible to see the other buildings at all from the street. The garage, the pool house and the gardener's cottage were all hidden away inside the ten-acre tract.

Sharley paused beside an intricately worked wrought-iron gate and dug through the pocket of her portfolio for the key. This side entrance to the estate had been seldom used in the past few years, but it was the quickest way to the gardener's cottage—the simple, solid little house that Charlotte and Martin had so generously renovated for the newlyweds.

And I might as well drop this little bombshell of Amy's off there now, Sharley told herself, and not risk having to explain it to Aunt Charlotte.

If Charlotte, bless her Victorian heart, saw that black lace negligee, she would definitely be shocked. And Sharley simply couldn't walk in with a package and not show her aunt the contents—Charlotte would be hurt. She was almost like a bride herself these days in her enjoyment of all Sharley's gifts and plans and arrangements.

Besides, if she stopped at the cottage, Sharley could check on whether the rest of the furniture had come today as promised. And, even more important, Spence might be there, too. He had said he might bring some things over from his apartment after work, now that the carpenters and the painters were done.

Just thinking of Spence brought soft warmth to her face. Perhaps they could have a little private time. Of course, in just another week, they'd have all the hours in the world together, but that knowledge didn't satisfy her today. It wasn't that she was jealous of him exactly, or unwilling to share him with the rest of the world. But right now everything was so busy and complicated there never seemed to be enough time. It would be nice just to sit down with him on their brand-new leather love seat and nestle into his arms and talk for a little while. Or not talk, perhaps, she thought with a smile, remembering the way he had kissed her good-night just last evening.

The cottage resembled an oversize playhouse. Like the main house, it was low and built of pale gray brick. Its most prominent features were a bay window and the front door, its burgundy paint still smelling fresh and new.

Automatically Sharley checked the bronze mailbox beside the front door. The box had always been intended more for looks than actual use. Since the estate gates were always locked, the real box was at the main entrance, and this one had been full of ancient cobwebs on the day she and Spence had first looked at the cottage. Perhaps that was why she had gotten the playful notion to use it for private kinds of messages.

There was an envelope in the box, and as she pulled it out she felt a mixture of glee and sadness. She always liked the notes Spence left—they were fresh and funny and charming. But the fact he'd put this here meant that he had already come and gone, and she was disappointed at missing him. He must have left work early. If only she hadn't stayed so long over her lesson plans!

She pushed the envelope into her coat pocket and unlocked the door, cautious not to mar the still-curing paint. The first thing she noticed as she walked through the tiny foyer and into the cozy living room was the leather love seat. The delivery men had set it at an awkward angle, with its back to the door rather than neatly perpendicular to the fireplace, as she intended to place it. But that would be easy enough to fix.

The second thing she saw was the back of Spence's head. He was sitting on the love seat, and there was no mistaking the stubborn wave of his dark brown hair or the aristocratic shape of his head...

Or the mass of long, shiny, black, feminine hair that lay against his shoulder.

Sharley opened her mouth, but her vocal cords seemed to have turned to cement.

In the instant she stood there, paralyzed and unable to breathe, Spence said, ''It can't go on like this, Wendy.'' His voice was low and husky.

The name was no surprise. Sharley had recognized that magnificent mane of black hair; after all, she had seen it less than an hour ago in the photograph on her desk. Even in an out-of-focus picture, or with her eyes blurred by angry tears, there was no mistaking Spence's secretary.

Doesn't she bother you? Amy had asked this after-noon. The question had sounded careless, but had it been? Sharley could feel the blood hammering in her ears. Did Amy know something, or suspect? Did everyone in Ham-mond's Point know that Spence Greenfield was carrying on with his secretary? Everyone, that is, but Sharley?

She tried out her voice again. This time it worked. "I got your note, Spence."

The love seat rocked backward as Spence leapt to his feet and wheeled to face her.

Sharley looked him over very slowly. He had taken off his jacket and tie. The collar of his shirt was loose, and his sleeves were rolled up. The color had drained from his face, and the cleft in his chin seemed to have gotten deeper. But he was no less handsome than before, for his good looks lay in his bones and the beautiful big gray eyes.

Only there wasn't any humorous twinkle in them now.

She took a step forward and rested her hand on the smooth leather and looked down at Wendy Taylor. The woman was wearing a red silk dressing gown and, appar-ently, nothing else.

At least it's not one of mine, Sharley thought.

She looked at Spence again. "Did you think if you left a note that I'd just trot on over to the main house, instead of coming into the cottage?"

"Sharley." He sounded as if something had hit him very hard just beneath the ribs.

Sharley's voice was starting to shake as fury burned through the first shock. "Dammit, Spence! In our own house. Our own love seat!"

"Sharley, please." He put out a hand. "I can explain."

The woman on the love seat clutched at his sleeve. There was panic on her face. "No, you can't, Spence."

He looked down at Wendy and bit his lip.

"There seems to be a difference of opinion," Sharley said with acid sweetness. "And though I hate to say it, I agree with Wendy on this one. I don't see how you can explain it. But I'm listening. Let's hear it."

Spence was silent. He shifted from one foot to the other and cleared his throat. But he didn't speak.

"Nothing at all to say?" Sharley's voice was almost gentle. "I guess I'm not surprised." She turned her back on him, walked to the burgundy door and shut it very firmly behind her, then ran down the narrow path toward the main house. Her lungs were aching from the exertion by the time she burst into the front hallway and slammed the door. She flung her coat and portfolio into the guest closet without caring how they landed and took the two stairs into the sunken living room with a leap.

From the solarium, around the corner and just out of sight, Charlotte Hudson said, "Sharley, dear, a lady does not bang doors like that."

Sharley pulled herself up short. She couldn't behave this way and expect Charlotte not to get upset and demand an explanation. And just now, the last thing she wanted to do was try to explain something to Aunt Charlotte that she didn't even begin to comprehend herself. If only she could get to her room. If only she could think this through before she had to face anyone at all...

She was to have no such luxury. An instant later, the front door was flung open and Spence gasped, "Dammit, Sharley, won't you even listen to me?"

Sharley spun around to face him. His hair was disheveled. From the wind? she wondered, or had Wendy run her fingers through it in an effort to keep him beside her?

"Have you had a chance to dream up a story? I thought perhaps you were still arguing with Wendy about whether you should even try to explain."

Spence rubbed the nape of his neck.

"I don't know how in the hell you expect me to believe that was innocent, Spence. I know what I saw!"

Charlotte Hudson came around the corner from the solarium, leaning heavily on a carved ebony walking stick. "Sharley, dear," she said sternly. "Really, I must protest your tone of voice. A lady does not allow herself to sound like a fishwife!"

"No matter what the circumstances, Aunt Charlotte?" She saw the shock in Spence's eyes and raised her chin a little. "I suppose I should be pleased that I didn't catch you with her in our bed, Spence. Except of course you couldn't—because it hasn't been delivered yet, has it?"

Charlotte put one hand to her temple and moaned.

Sharley was horrified at herself for forgetting, even for an instant, Charlotte's less-than-robust health. She yelled for the housekeeper. Libby appeared so promptly that Sharley thought she must have been leaning against the kitchen door listening to the scene.

The housekeeper helped Charlotte over to the couch, where she sank down against the cushions and murmured, "Martin. Get Martin, please. He's in the garden somewhere."

But Martin Hudson had followed Libby from the kitchen. He was wearing his gardening clothes and a faded, shapeless old fishing hat. He bent over his wife and took her limp hand between his. "There, there, Charlotte," he murmured. "Just don't fret so. Take a deep breath and relax."

Charlotte was really upset, Sharley thought. She hadn't even mentioned to Martin that he should take his hat off in the house.

Sharley was heartily ashamed of herself even for thinking that way. Of course Charlotte was distressed; she had good reason to be. And she was correct about one thing, at least—screaming was no way to handle this problem.

Sharley squared her shoulders and turned to face Spence. He was standing on the topmost of the shallow steps leading down to the living room almost as if he was balanced on the very edge of it.

"I'm listening," she said. "So explain."

Spence swallowed hard and looked from her to the little group by the couch. There was a silent plea in his eyes as he turned back to Sharley.

She said quietly, "They don't know the details yet, but under the circumstances what happened will have to come out, Spence. I wouldn't shelter you from it even if I could. You might as well explain it to them right now, too." Her voice cracked a little. "So tell me, Spence. Why were you in our cottage with a half-naked woman in your arms?"

She found herself holding her breath. As damning as the scene had been, was there some innocent explanation for Wendy's presence at the cottage, for her state of undress, for what Spence had said to her?

He looked toward Martin and Charlotte again, and took a single step down toward Sharley. He was very pale, and his face was set like a stone mask. "Trust me, Sharley. It's not what you think."

That was all. She waited while the silence dragged out into forever, while Martin fanned his wife's face with a magazine and the housekeeper went running for a glass of water. And when a full minute had gone by and it was obvious that Spence had said everything he intended to, Sharley reached deep into herself for strength and said calmly, "*That's* what you call an explanation? Just 'Trust me, Sharley'?"

He didn't move. "It's the only one I can give you."

"And you say it's not what I think," she mused. "Isn't that what every man says when he gets caught red-handed? I expected something a little more creative from you, Spence."

She had not thought it possible for him to get whiter, but he did. "Do you love me, Sharley?" His voice was low.

Of course she loved him. She was going to marry him.

She wet her lips. "What has that got to do with it?"

It was obvious he heard the tiny quaver in her voice. "If you care for me at all . . ."

"Then it doesn't matter what you did?" She could feel her self-control slipping and hysteria building in the pit of her stomach.

"You'd take my word for it, if you loved me enough."

"If I loved you enough? How dare you make it sound as if I'm the one who's fallen short?" She bit her lip hard. "But you're right, Spence. If you can't explain, I don't think I love you enough to take your word for this."

His eyes hardened to dark steel. "Then it's better to find out now, isn't it?"

"Certainly." Sharley didn't spare a glance for her diamond ring—the ring she had been so proud of—as she pulled it from her finger.

Spence made no move to reach for it and she didn't think she could bear to touch him, so she dropped the ring onto a granite-topped table at the foot of the shallow steps. It spun a little, the fine gold vibrating against the cold stone before it was still.

He waited till she had turned away, then came down the last step, scooped up the ring and dropped it carelessly into his shirt pocket. "Don't bother to come to the door," he said crisply. "I'll see myself out."

By the time Sharley had wheeled around to snap at him, he was gone.

It was just as well, she thought. There was nothing left worth saying, anyway.

CHAPTER TWO

THE SLAM of the great walnut front door reverberated through the house until it seemed to Sharley that the windows would shatter under the strain.

Martin winced at the sound and looked sternly at Sharley. "What the hell is going on here?" he demanded.

Charlotte said, "Martin, please watch your language."

Sharley knelt beside the couch. "I'm sorry, Aunt Charlotte. I didn't mean for this to distress you." She took a deep breath. "I guess I just— The shock was too much."

"The shock of what?" Martin asked irritably.

"Finding Spence with a woman, of course," Charlotte said. "What's the matter with you, Martin? Didn't you hear?" She raised a thin white hand to pat Sharley's cheek. "I understand completely, my dear. Of course you were shocked."

"I'm sure there's an explanation for it," Martin said.

"Don't be naive. Certainly there's an explanation—the obvious one." Charlotte moved restlessly. "If you will help me to sit up now..."

Martin didn't seem to hear. "Spence? With a woman? Sharley, when you've both had a chance to cool down, you'll probably find it was all a silly misunderstanding."

"Don't be ridiculous." Charlotte's voice was coming back to normal now. "Sharley has done the only thing she could under the circumstances—dismissing the young man. Now, if you will offer me your arm, Martin—"

"Charlotte, they haven't even talked about it!"

Sharley couldn't believe what she was hearing. She had just walked in on her fiancé in the arms of another woman, and Martin and Charlotte were coming to blows over it! It was *her* engagement that had just fallen apart, *her* wedding that would have to be called off, and they...

She began to tremble as the full weight of what had happened descended on her shoulders. There was not only a wedding to be canceled, but a marriage.

Martin patted her arm sympathetically. "You consider it, honey, and don't jump to any conclusions. We'll just sit here and talk it over, and once you're calmer I'll give Spence a call and get him back here."

"Please," Sharley said desperately. "I appreciate your concern, but I'd really like to be alone for a while."

Martin looked hurt.

Charlotte struggled to a sitting position on the couch. "Of course, dear," she said. "Go and rest. I'll send Libby along with something to help you relax."

Sharley didn't answer. She had to focus every scrap of her mind just to get across the enormous living room, up the two steps and along the hallway to her bedroom. She shut her door behind her and leaned against it with a sigh of relief.

They meant well, she told herself. She shouldn't be surprised that Martin wanted to take the problem apart and analyze it, or that Charlotte's first instinct was to medicate the difficulty out of existence. They had never understood that not all problems could be analyzed or ignored.

Sometimes, Sharley thought, they just have to be survived.

She was shivering so badly that she could hardly pull the hand-quilted comforter off the brass rack at the foot of her bed. Heedless of the satin spread, she sank down on the mattress and pulled the comforter awkwardly around her, huddling into its warmth. It didn't help much; she felt as if her bones were frozen.

It wasn't that Martin and Charlotte didn't love her; Sharley knew they did. But they had never had children of their own and so had never learned a lesson most parents learned as their children grew up—that sometimes what was needed wasn't analysis or advice, and certainly not avoidance, but just a comforting pat on the back and a shoulder to cry on.

Great, Sharley thought. A little more of this and she would be so deep in self-pity she'd be wishing she'd never been born.

Libby tapped on the door and came in carrying a glass of water and a couple of tablets. Sharley sat up and took the water, but shook her head at the medication. Charlotte had enough varieties of tranquillizers and sleeping pills to stock a pharmacy, and Sharley recognized these as among the stronger ones. They'd knock her out till tomorrow morning, but what would that solve?

"I didn't think you'd want them," the housekeeper said, "but Mrs. Hudson insisted."

"I'd just be putting the pain off till tomorrow."

"Sometimes that's not a bad idea," Libby pointed out gently. "I'll leave these here in case you change your mind, and I'll bring your dinner in later."

Sharley shook her head. "That would just make more work for you, Libby."

"You can't quit eating."

"I'll come out." Sharley tried to smile. "I have to face the music sometime. I might as well do it tonight, while I'm still numb."

"Good thing you were almost grown when you came to live with them," the housekeeper mused. "They'd have ruined you otherwise, fussing over every tear and every case of hurt feelings. Not that this is a little thing exactly. But you'll come through it all right." Her step was so quiet that she was almost to the door before Sharley realized she was leaving.

"Libby!" she called. As the woman turned, one eyebrow raised inquiringly, Sharley cleared her throat. "Thank you. For having confidence in me, I mean."

"You're strong and you're sensible, Sharley. You'll find your way through this."

Sharley smiled a little. Aunt Charlotte would have had an attack if she'd heard that flat and unemotional assessment, and she probably would have scolded Libby for being unsympathetic. Sharley, on the other hand, found Libby's quiet conviction reassuring, something to live up to.

Spence would appreciate the ironic humor of that contrast, too, Sharley thought idly. She'd have to tell him about it....

Then reality swept over her. For a few seconds, she'd actually forgotten that she wasn't likely to be telling Spence anything more at all.

She tried to swallow the choking pain in her throat, but without success. *Spence,* she thought. *How could you do this to me?*

Sharley stared at the ceiling. As dusk settled across the estate, the ornamental lights in the garden came on one by one. Each cast long shadows of the nearby branches through her window shades and onto the delicate tracings in the plaster ceiling. The shadows moved silently, overlapping and merging in confusing patterns—patterns like the ones in Sharley's mind.

If there had been any sensible explanation, why hadn't Spence offered it right there in the cottage? On the other hand, if there wasn't an explanation, why had he chased Sharley to the main house? But then, if he had any excuse at all, why hadn't he offered it once he caught up with her? Why had he said only, *Trust me, Sharley . . . ?*

"Dammit," Sharley said crossly. "It's ridiculous to torment myself this way!" If there had been any justification for Spence's behavior, he'd have given it. Since he hadn't, there wasn't any justification. It was as simple as that.

One thing was certain. He had acted—and sounded—as guilty as any man could be.

And yet, he had managed to make it seem as if he was the innocent party. As if Sharley was the one in the wrong!

She tried to shake away the feeling of guilt that nagged at her. It was completely irrational for her to feel guilty, she told herself. Spence had been caught almost in the act—and he obviously felt so bad about it that he couldn't face up to what he'd done. So to excuse his behavior he had to blame someone else. He was probably thinking that if Sharley hadn't walked in, there wouldn't have been a problem. Therefore it was *her* fault.

On the other hand, he had certainly told Wendy that the affair couldn't go on; perhaps he had honestly felt that made the whole thing none of Sharley's business.

The explanation was simple, and it even made a crazy kind of sense. And yet, she thought, that kind of thinking was so unlike Spence. He wasn't one to duck responsibility or sidle away from difficult situations. The Spence Greenfield she knew . . .

Sharley drew herself up short and asked herself somberly, *Do I really know Spence at all?*

LIBBY HAD WAITED till the last possible moment before tapping on Sharley's door to tell her dinner was served, so

Charlotte and Martin were already seated when Sharley came in. She knew they'd been talking about her, of course, for their conversation broke off awkwardly the second she stepped into the dining room.

Martin jumped up to hold her chair with even more than his usual solicitousness, and Charlotte toyed with her crisp linen napkin and waited until he was settled in his chair again before she picked up her soup spoon.

Sharley followed suit, though she expected the rich, creamy vichyssoise would probably choke her.

Martin shook out his napkin with a snap, which made Charlotte frown. "The crocus are up, Sharley, and the daffodils are peeking through, too. I was just telling Charlotte."

The tightness in Sharley's throat relaxed just a little. Bless Uncle Martin, she thought, for trying to make things a bit easier. She smiled at him, thinking what a contrast he was, in his blue velvet smoking jacket, to the disreputable-looking grubby gardener of this afternoon. He had never made much effort to hide his age; in fact, his steel-gray hair and the lines in his face lent him a certain appeal, which was absent in the photographs of him as a young man.

Charlotte, on the other hand, had been trying for years to deny the passage of time. Her hair was always carefully tinted and coiffed, her nails manicured and her makeup in the latest mode. In the past few months she had even taken to wearing high necklines to conceal the inevitable effect of gravity on her throat.

Occasionally Sharley couldn't help being amused by some of her aunt's wilder attempts to hang on to youth, but mostly she felt sad. Charlotte's ill health had robbed her of so many things. Beauty was the least of them.

There was a fretful little line between Charlotte's brows now, and Sharley saw that her aunt wasn't eating much, either.

Sharley put down her spoon, grateful for the excuse to stop trying to swallow. "If you don't mind," she said quietly, "I'd just as soon get this discussion behind us. I know you both got the general idea this afternoon, but perhaps I should tell you that Spence was in the cottage—"

"Right here on the estate?" Charlotte asked sharply.

Sharley nodded. "And the woman..." She paused. If she told Martin her name, Wendy Taylor would no doubt be out of a job by tomorrow morning.

But even if she wanted to protect Wendy, there wasn't any way to keep that fact under wraps; Hammond's Point was too small a town to keep secrets of that caliber. Charlotte would not rest easy until she knew who the woman was, and then her first move would be to tell Martin, so it made no difference whether or not Sharley kept silent.

Of course, it wouldn't be any surprise if half the town already suspected what had been going on. It would undoubtedly be better to tell Charlotte the truth now than to let her ask the members of her bridge club, who might even gloat—with sympathetic overtones, of course—about Sharley's shortsightedness. And it would certainly be better to tell Martin he had a problem in his executive offices than to let him hear the facts from his golf buddies.

Sharley looked down at her soup and said quietly, "The woman was his secretary."

"Wendy Taylor?" Charlotte said. "Why, the little hussy! I told you she was no good, Martin. But I must say I'm surprised at Spence—putting Hudson Products at risk like that when you've given him such a wonderful opportunity."

That was a side of the equation Sharley had not looked at before. For Spence to be involved with any woman was bad enough, Charlotte seemed to be saying, but for him to mess around where his job was concerned was really crazy.

She could understand Charlotte's point. Still, she thought, it doesn't matter much to me whether it's Wendy or my best friend or some bimbo I don't even know!

Sharley glanced at Martin. His normally ruddy cheeks were pale, and for the first time in all the years she'd known him, his voice quavered like that of an old man. "I'll speak to Spence in the morning," he said almost to himself.

Sharley stared at him in surprised disappointment. Obviously he, too, was suddenly finding the situation even more critical than he had thought at first. It was almost as if Sharley's feelings were not important at all beside this threat to the integrity of Hudson Products.

A moment later, sanity reasserted itself. For the past couple of years, ever since Spence had come to work for Hudson Products, Martin had been grooming him to take over the firm someday. Now that Spence's judgment had been so harshly called into question, of course Martin would consider the additional impact on the business. He would hardly be human if he didn't. His reaction didn't belittle his concern for Sharley, but he loved Spence, too.

Like the son he'd never had, Sharley thought.

Before she spoke, she had considered the almost certain consequences to Wendy. But it hadn't occurred to her to wonder if this was going to cost Spence his job, as well.

Why should that bother her? Sharley asked herself. All she'd done was tell the truth. She wasn't the one who'd made the bad choices; Spence had done that by himself. If he really had no idea of the severity and stupidity of this lapse, then he deserved to lose his position, didn't he?

The argument didn't soothe the sick feeling in the pit of her stomach.

Quietly and efficiently, Libby cleared the almost untouched soup plates and brought in the main course. Sharley looked at the tiny elegant lamb chops and baby vegetables in a picture-perfect array on the china plate and thought she would probably never be able to face that combination again.

Charlotte picked up her knife and fork. "I am disappointed, of course," she said. "I thought Spence was more stable than that. Though I suppose it's not surprising, with his father being what he was, for him to be—"

"That's ridiculous, Charlotte," Martin interrupted. "John Greenfield was a fool, but that doesn't mean Spence is, too."

"John Greenfield was also a cheat and a liar," Charlotte said crisply. "And he could charm the devil into believing his stories. Say what you will, Martin, there is a taint in families sometimes. Perhaps it's just as well that it's come out into the open now, before..."

Charlotte paused, but it was obvious she was thinking, *before there's another generation to carry on the hereditary weakness.*

Sharley closed her eyes for a moment, trying to ward off the raw pain that ripped through her body. "If you will excuse me, please, Aunt Charlotte," she began, "I don't think I..." She pushed back her chair.

As she left the dining room, she heard Charlotte add, "In any case, Martin, when a woman provides the money in a marriage she has the right to call the shots. Whatever else Spence might be, he isn't very wise not to have realized that, you know."

Sharley stumbled on the steps to the bedroom wing. *When a woman provides the money...*

"Oh, no," she whispered. "Please, dear heaven, not that."

Sharley had always known, in the back of her mind, that Martin and Charlotte intended her to benefit from their wealth. Even before her parents had died, that much had been clear, though it had never been openly discussed. She was their only niece. Of course they would provide for her.

And after she had come to live with them, they had done exactly that. They had paid her tuition at an expensive private college. They had given her a car. And she had quickly learned to be cautious of what she admired, because more times than not if she said she liked something, one of them would buy it for her.

Now and then, Martin had spoken to her about investments and safe yields, and Charlotte had instructed her about charities and good works and the social responsibility money represented.

But they had never given her any details about their plans or their wills or what would eventually happen to their wealth. Sharley had listened politely to the lectures but assumed that, like much of what Martin and Charlotte said, this was overkill. When all was said and done, she expected most of their money would go to the charities they had so faithfully supported over the years. And that was just fine with her; in Sharley's opinion, the Hudsons had done quite enough for her as it was. They had equipped her to make her way in the world, and they continued to give her a home.

But was she being naive? Did they intend to leave her every dime they possessed? Was that why Spence Greenfield had suddenly become so interested in her last Christmas?

SHARLEY SPENT MOST of Saturday afternoon on the telephone, canceling the arrangements for the wedding. The caterer, the florist, the organist, the manager of the country club, each of them was stunned by her request and insisted that Sharley say it again before the news actually sank in. By the time she had finished repeating the endlessly agonizing sentences, she was trembling from the effort. And she couldn't help thinking that on this perfect afternoon she should have been playing golf with Spence, or unpacking wedding gifts at the cottage...with Spence....

She choked back the tears and cradled her head in her hands for a moment. She'd take a break, she decided, and make herself a cup of tea with honey to soothe the ache in her throat. Then she'd work her way down the long list of invited guests to let them know the wedding was off.

Charlotte had offered to help with that duty. But she'd looked wan and weak this morning, as if she hadn't slept at all, and Sharley thought that nosy questions were likely to do her no good. There would be plenty of those for all of them to face in the next few weeks; no need for Charlotte to go looking for more.

Sharley started for the kitchen to brew her tea. Preoccupied with the incredible number of calls she had yet to make, she was actually in the solarium before she heard the murmur of voices, and she stopped abruptly just inside the door. "Excuse me, Aunt Charlotte," she managed. "I didn't realize you had guests."

Three ladies were grouped around Charlotte's chaise lounge. Each was as well-groomed and sleek as Charlotte herself, and each looked at Sharley with barely restrained curiosity.

Word travels fast, Sharley thought. The other half of the bridge club would no doubt be dropping in any minute.

She wondered what their excuses were for stopping by to see Charlotte on a Saturday afternoon.

Her aunt waved a thin hand at a nearby chair. "Come and join us, darling."

Sharley shook her head. "Thank you, but I've got a lot of phone calls to make. I was just going through to the kitchen."

"Then would you tell Libby we'd like coffee now?" Charlotte asked.

As Sharley retreated through the dining room, she heard one of her aunt's visitors murmur, "The poor darling. She's being so brave, isn't she?"

"I'm glad she has a vacation coming up," Charlotte said. "She'll feel better when the pressure of school is let up for a while."

As if that was going to help, Sharley thought. She'd just have more time to think then, and to remember that she should have been in Nassau, basking on a beach—with Spence.

Libby was bustling about the kitchen setting up a tray with the big silver coffeepot. "I know," she said crisply, just as Sharley opened her mouth. "When they came, I was making a raspberry shortcake for the scholarship fund-raiser, and I couldn't stop in the middle. So now I'm rushing to catch up. There're some chocolate baskets up in that cabinet. Would you put a scoop of ice cream in each of them while I wash the rest of the raspberries?"

Sharley was relieved to have her hands busy. She unwrapped each delicate chocolate confection, set it carefully on a crystal dessert plate and added a generous dollop of rich vanilla ice cream.

Martin came in from the garden before she was finished, smelling of damp earth and peat moss.

"Don't go in," Libby warned. "The bridge ladies are here."

"On Saturday?" Martin eyed the desserts. "Those look awfully good."

Sharley pointed with her ice-cream scoop at a chocolate basket that had fallen apart as she'd unwrapped it. "There's a broken one if you want to nibble. Or, if you'll be patient a minute, I'll make you a super-special dessert as soon as these are done."

Martin pushed his hat back off his forehead, picked up the defective bit of chocolate and began snapping it into bite-sized bits. "This is fine. Come out into the garden with me for a while, Sharley."

"Thanks, but I'm afraid I'm not exactly in the mood to commune with crocus today, Uncle Martin." She filled the last basket, then leaned against the refrigerator and licked the ice-cream scoop, studying him suspiciously. "Why? Have you got Spence hidden in the boxwood or something?" There was a strange sensation in her stomach, as if she was a spring-powered toy that had been wound too tight. Martin had been gone all morning. Was it possible . . . ?

Martin shot a look at Libby and then shook his head.

The spring inside Sharley seemed to pop and sag and lose its power.

Libby sprinkled fresh raspberries across each scoop of ice cream and picked up the tray. She backed through the swinging door and disappeared toward the solarium.

"I talked to him," Martin said, then stopped as if he didn't quite know where to go from there.

"I take it that means he didn't have any explanations for you, either? Have you finally realized this is not just a silly misunderstanding?"

Martin looked miserable.

Sharley was ashamed of herself. "I'm sorry, Uncle Martin. I know you're trying to help."

"If you'd only talk to him, Sharley..."

"Does that mean you couldn't convince him to make the first move, so you're back to trying to persuade me? Uncle Martin, when it comes right down to it, Spence is the one who walked out on me. I gave him the opportunity to explain yesterday, but he didn't seem to want it."

Martin opened his mouth and then shut it again, like a helpless goldfish.

Sharley put her arms around him and buried her head in the shoulder of his faded old flannel shirt. "I'm sorry to sound like such a bear." Her voice was muffled. "All the things you and Charlotte have done for me, and this is the way I reward you." She swallowed hard. "It's not that I'm refusing to talk to him, you know, but I suspect Spence isn't exactly eager to talk to me, either. Is he?"

"Stupid young fool," Martin said under his breath.

"Well, there you have it, don't you?" Sharley dashed moisture from the corner of her eyes and tried to smile. "Which one of us are you calling a stupid young fool, by the way?"

Martin took a deep breath. "Sharley—"

Libby returned to the kitchen. "One of them has to have artificial sweetener," she was muttering under her breath as she began rummaging through a drawer. "She's spooning up ice cream as if it's nothing at all, but she can't stand a bit of sugar in her coffee."

Sharley smiled a little. "It's not like you to be so impatient with Aunt Charlotte's guests, Libby."

The housekeeper darted her a look. "Oh, it's not the sweetener," she admitted. "It's the way they're talking about you that annoys me. Mrs. Hudson can't see through that fake sympathy to the catty gossip underneath, that's the real pity. She ought to just throw them out."

Sharley sighed. "They're her friends, and I can't blame them for being curious. But it's going to be a very long spring break, I'm afraid."

"Maybe you ought to go to the Bahamas, anyway," Libby said as she dumped artificial sweetener into a crystal bowl. "Why shouldn't you enjoy your time off, wedding or no wedding?" She moved swiftly across the kitchen, and the swinging door dropped shut behind her.

"What a singular honeymoon that would be," Sharley murmured. The idea had a certain farcical appeal, she had to admit. But by the time she made her tea and went back to her room to take up her telephone list again, she had forgotten the whole crazy notion.

Martin, however, had obviously passed the idea on to Charlotte, for she brought it up over dinner. "It's a very sensible plan, Sharley," she said as she drank her consommé.

"To go on my honeymoon by myself? Aunt Charlotte—"

"Why not? It's too late to cancel the reservations, so you may as well get some good of it. Besides, it's not as if Spence had anything to do with the arrangements. The resort was a gift to you from Martin and me."

"It was a gift to *us*," Sharley murmured. "I hardly think—"

Charlotte went straight on. "Why waste a good vacation?"

"Are you implying I should pick up the first handsome man I see on the beach? Honestly, Aunt Charlotte!"

Charlotte sat up even straighter, and her voice was like ice. "Of course not."

Sharley bit her lip. "I beg your pardon."

Charlotte unbent slightly, but the atmosphere remained on the cool side, despite Martin's efforts. Sharley was almost glad to be able to excuse herself just after the main course, reminding Charlotte of her commitment to help serve desserts at the scholarship fund-raiser.

"And to think I'm actually glad to be going out in public," she muttered to herself. Well, she had to face it sometime, and considering the prompt response of the bridge ladies, it was going to be sooner rather than later. It was astounding how fast gossip traveled in a town this size. She'd just keep her chin up and smile, that was all.

But she couldn't help thinking that it was too bad she and Spence hadn't at least agreed on a story that would allow them both to keep their dignity. She didn't intend to lie about it, exactly, but it would be so much better not to have the details slung all over Hammond's Point.

After all, she thought, both of them still had to live there.

THE RECEPTION WASN'T as bad as she'd expected; though there were plenty of sympathetic and curious comments, only one woman came straight out and asked why Sharley's engagement had come to such a crashing end.

Almost automatically Sharley gave the same answer she had used on the telephone all day. "Spence and I have concluded that we are not well suited, after all."

"Now, really," the woman urged. "There's obviously more to it than that."

Sharley looked straight through her. "How kind of you to be so concerned," she said coolly.

Amy Howell appeared beside her at that moment, coffee cup in hand. "Now that the crowd has died down, we can talk over lesson plans for next week, Sharley." She smiled sweetly at the inquisitive woman, who sniffed and moved off.

"Thank you," Sharley murmured. "That was almost as effective as giving her a kick."

"Which I wouldn't have minded doing. How do you feel?"

There was no need to tell social fibs to Amy, Sharley thought with relief. When Amy asked how someone was, she really wanted to know. "As if a grand piano just fell out of nowhere and hit me on the head."

Amy's hand came to rest for just a moment atop Sharley's, with a comforting squeeze. "I couldn't believe it when you called today."

"Did you know about Wendy when you asked yesterday if it bothered me that she's Spence's secretary?"

Amy shook her head. "Not a hint, I swear. I just always thought that having a woman like Wendy around was looking for trouble. Heavens, I sound like a Puritan, don't I? The women's movement would read me out of the organization." She sipped her coffee. "Are you going to be in school Monday?"

"Of course. Why wouldn't I be?"

Amy shrugged. "I didn't know if your nerves would stand the stress, on top of everything else."

"Frankly I'm looking forward to the stress. I can't afford to let my thoughts wander with the kids around, so I'll have to put this out of my mind. It's March break I'm not looking forward to."

"Well, if you get too frazzled, just run up the white flag. I'll take your kids into my room for math games or something and give you a chance to regroup."

"You're a love, Amy."

"And as far as the break is concerned, it's not too late to come along on our skiing trip."

Sharley swallowed hard. "That's very thoughtful, but taking me along would be a real imposition."

"Not really. We're driving to Colorado, and we've rented a condo. We can fit one more in with no trouble. Just bring a sleeping bag."

"Thanks, but I don't think so, Amy. The last thing I need is to spend the rest of the school year with a twisted knee from going down a ski slope wrong."

Amy moved aside so an elderly man could step up to the table. Sharley cut a slice from the kiwifruit tart he pointed to, slid it onto a plate and handed it to him with a smile.

Amy shrugged. "At least a twisted knee would give you a good excuse to hang around the whirlpool..."

Sharley didn't hear the rest. As the man turned away with his kiwifruit tart, she saw Spence appear in the doorway, and her body tightened as if someone had slid a knife between her ribs.

My Lord, how much I've missed him, she thought. It's only been a day....

He looked taller, somehow, in his dark suit. Sharley had grown used to seeing him in sports coats and blazers and sweaters, not pinstripes, and the contrast made her feel somehow as if she hadn't seen him at all in a long, long time. The charcoal suit made his eyes even deeper and more lustrous.

Or were those changes caused not by the color of his clothes but the woman who stood beside him? Wendy Taylor, with one small hand clutching Spence's sleeve, the other tight on a tiny black velvet evening bag that matched her dainty cocktail dress, and looking straight at Sharley—not in triumph, but almost as if she felt sympathy!

Sharley's anger seemed to start at the tip of her toes and burn its way upward, cell by cell. Couldn't he even have the decency to wait a few days to flaunt Wendy? Just a few days, till the grapevine found something else to exclaim over? Only Sharley and Spence and Wendy knew the details. Only they *ever* needed to know, unless it was Spence's intention to feed the gossip.

She looked down at the array of desserts on the table before her. Her fingers were actually shaking with the desire to pick up the nearest one—the sweet, sticky remains of Libby's raspberry shortcake—and grind it into Spence's face.

"Well, if you change your mind about the skiing trip," Amy said, "just let me know. We don't mind a last-minute decision."

Amy's words seemed to be coming from a long way off. Sharley shook her head. "I've already decided what to do over March break." Her voice was clear and vibrant, and no one within ten feet of the dessert table could help but hear. "I'm going to the Bahamas, anyway."

A collective gasp rippled through the room, followed by a momentary silence.

Amy said skeptically, "Alone?"

"Of course I'm going alone," Sharley said. She looked directly at Spence and raised her chin a fraction of an inch. "Frankly, my dear, compared to what I'd originally planned, being alone will be a blessing."

CHAPTER THREE

THE IDEA WAS CRAZY, of course, and Sharley had no intention of actually doing any such thing. A jilted bride going on a honeymoon by herself? It was ridiculous. If it hadn't been for that sympathetic look of Wendy's—that glance that said so clearly, I've got him and you don't, and I'm sorry for you!—Sharley would have kept her peace and minded her manners and not said anything at all.

Still, as the week wore on, she found herself thinking more and more often about getting away. It would be soothing to go where no one knew about Spence, where no one would question why Sharley was no longer half of a pair. And by the time she came home, perhaps the gossips of Hammond's Point would have moved on to some other juicy tidbit.

One of those urges to pack up and leave hit her on Sunday morning, when the announcement was made in church. It was just a simple statement, one more reminder in a long list, made without emphasis by the clergyman who would have performed the ceremony. "The wedding of Sharley Collins and Spence Greenfield, planned for next Saturday, will not take place," he said calmly, and moved straight on to the ladies' auxiliary meeting.

The murmur of surprise that rippled through the sanctuary startled Sharley, who'd have sworn that no one in Hammond's Point could possibly have failed to hear the news by now. What startled her even more was her own reaction. Her palms began to sweat, her heartbeat accelerated, and she felt as if she was smothering. She was suffering a classic panic attack, she told herself, as though the announcement was news to her, too. Somehow the pastor's calm statement seemed to make painful reality of something that until then had been too much a nightmare to be faced at all.

But that was not the only thing that made her long to get away. On Tuesday after school, Charlotte took a good look at Sharley's nails and exclaimed, "Good heavens, you're not biting them again, are you?"

Sharley explained how the combination of tempera paint and clay had worked its way so deeply under her nails during art class that day that the only option was to cut them short. But for a moment she wasn't sure whether Charlotte really believed her, and that annoyed her even more. If she'd actually been biting her nails again, Sharley would have admitted it. It wasn't a crime, after all.

On Wednesday, one of the innocents in her classroom asked whether "forbidden fruit" was apples or pears or grapes, and when Sharley pressed for the reason for the question, the child said, "My mommy said you're not getting married because your boyfriend couldn't stay away from forbidden fruit. It can't be bananas, because Mommy likes for me to eat them. Is it oranges? She says I should only have one of those a day." The girl looked puzzled. "Did he eat too many oranges? Is that why you won't marry him?"

Yes, Sharley thought wearily, going away for a while would be a very good idea.

But the crowning touch came on Thursday. After school let out, she stopped at the hardware store, one of the half-dozen places where she and Spence had so happily registered their gift list. Now she had to cancel those requests and arrange for the gifts to be credited to the sender and returned to the shelves. She had already taken care of those same details at the department stores and the kitchenware place, but she had left the hardware store for last, because she knew it would be the most difficult to face. In fact, she paused outside the door and swallowed hard, trying to work up her courage to even go inside.

The choice of china and crystal and silver had been Sharley's. Spence had looked at patterns with almost infinite patience, but finally he had declared that it didn't matter to him whether he ate from bone china or paper, since he intended to stare at his bride, not the dishes, anyway. Sharley had looked into his eyes and felt a familiar little sensation in the pit of her stomach—the same weightless feeling one got at the top of the first peak of a roller coaster—and she had fallen a little more in love with him.

So she had selected the china and crystal and silver, as well as the pots and pans. But at the hardware store Spence had been different. He had soberly studied the merits of cordless screwdrivers versus the ordinary hand-powered kind, and ended up putting both on his wish list. He had tried out each hammer, drill and saw in stock. He had been intrigued with an incredible array of gadgets. And when he insisted on testing every snow shovel in the place and finally selected one with a bent handle that was supposed to lessen back strain, Sharley couldn't keep silent any longer. "We don't even need a snow shovel, much less one with a fancy handle," she had pointed out. "The handyman takes care of clearing the sidewalks and the drive."

"Ah," Spence said without a flicker of a smile. "But what if he gets sick? I wouldn't want you to hurt your back while you dig your way to school."

Sharley punched him in the arm before she saw the teasing sparkle in his eyes, and Spence retaliated, kissing her unmercifully right there in the aisle between rakes and axes until she was gasping for breath.

It was a good thing that tidbit hadn't come to Aunt Charlotte's ears, Sharley thought, with a conspiratorial smile. She would have given Spence a good trimming over his lack of manners, kissing Sharley in public like that....

Her smile died. Letting herself think about how much she ached for his touch, how much she missed the warm security of his hugs, would not make things get better. So she pulled the door open...

...and walked straight into Spence.

The impact rocked her off balance, and Spence dropped the bag he was carrying in order to steady her. For a moment she was almost in his arms, his hands gripping her elbows, her face pressed against the rough tweed of his coat. Automatically she closed her eyes and inhaled, and the scent of his after-shave hit her brain with a rush that made her dizzy. It had always been her favorite brand, but when Spence wore it the chemistry changed somehow, till it wasn't merely a scent anymore but a sensation.

She looked up at him. Her eyes were precisely on a level with his chin, and she knew from experience that if she stood on her toes and leaned against him, she could just barely brush her lips against the deep cleft in his chin. The first time she had done that, he had looked startled—and then he had bent his head and kissed her breathless.

The memory still had the power to make her knees go weak.

Almost as if he had read her mind, Spence set her firmly back on her feet and released her.

He looked as if he'd been carved out of rock. There was no warmth in his eyes, no hint of humor at the corners of his mouth, where she had thought a smile always lurked. She bit her lip. She had never seen this cold, hard man before. If the episode in the gardener's cottage had done this to him...

But what made her think that the change in him was an emotional reaction to losing the woman he loved? she asked herself curtly. It could just as easily be fury with himself for messing up a perfect opportunity to marry a fortune, or anger at his own carelessness in getting caught. Perhaps Wendy was making demands on him. Or maybe Martin had finally made up his mind that Hudson Products could do without Spence Greenfield. But there wasn't any polite way to ask.

"If you came to cancel the gift registry," he said, "don't bother. I've already done it."

Sharley nodded, hardly hearing him, thinking that she couldn't stand not knowing. "Has Uncle Martin fired you?"

Spence's eyes narrowed to gunmetal-gray slits. "No, he hasn't. Your vengeance knows no bounds, does it, Sharley?"

She shook her head, then realized that the gesture could have more than one meaning. "No. I mean, that wasn't why I was asking." It hadn't been a tactful question, she admitted, but surely, if he hadn't been fired, there was no need for him to be so cold and curt about it.

He stared at her for one drawn-out moment, then bent to retrieve his bag. It had torn, and part of the contents had spilled out. He scooped up a bulky Swiss army knife and a container of touch-up paint the color of his car and dropped them into his pocket.

"I don't want you to lose your job, Spence."

He didn't seem to hear. He picked up a package of light bulbs and put it into what remained of the bag, then dropped a couple of fat green candles on top.

"You'll break those bulbs," Sharley warned.

"If they aren't shattered from the fall already." He tucked the bag under his arm. "Pardon me if I don't stay here and listen to the rest of the lecture. I have other things to do."

The door swung shut behind him. Sharley went back to her car and sat there for a long while, shaking.

For the past few days, school had provided her with some solace—a place to go, something to think about besides her own pain, physical activity to tire her body. But ahead of her lay a long and empty week, days that should have been the happiest of her life. If she ventured out, she might run into Spence again at any turn. If she stayed at home, she'd have Charlotte's solicitous care to deal with, and much as she loved her aunt, Sharley didn't think her sympathy would be a lot of comfort. In either case, the whole town would be watching as she struggled through the hours when she should have been celebrating her wedding rehearsal or dressing in that beautiful satin-and-lace gown or greeting her guests at her reception.

Getting away from it all had never looked so good.

She would not go to the Bahamas, of course. Going alone to the resort where they should have started a new life together wouldn't be any kind of comfort at all. But there were other places she could go.

She raised her head as the answer came to her. She would go to the cabin. No one would ever dream of looking for her there.

The only really surprising thing was that it had taken Sharley so long to think of it. But then, the cabin in the woods was Martin's; Charlotte did no more than tolerate the place. In fact, Sharley thought her aunt probably hadn't set foot in the cabin for years, and the subjects of hunting, fishing and camping so thoroughly bored his wife that Martin seldom even mentioned them.

Sharley, on the other hand, had gone with Martin a few times when she'd been in her teens. She had done her hunting with a pair of binoculars and declined to fish at all. She had loved that isolated spot in the woods, but in the past few years the timing never seemed right for her to go back. Either Sharley was in school or they were all off to some other place entirely, and somehow the cabin had dropped completely out of her mind.

But there, alone among the pines, she could think. She could cry if she needed to, and she could work things out. And if she was very lucky, she could find peace.

SHARLEY FELT like a world-class liar, but she told no one where she was actually going. When Charlotte offered to help choose which parts of her trousseau to take, Sharley declined with a smile, saying she didn't want her aunt to wear herself out. If Charlotte knew her niece was headed for an isolated clearing in the woods—alone—she'd have another stroke. Not telling her was a kindness of a sort.

When Libby commented on the fact that she hadn't packed a swimsuit, Sharley said uncomfortably that she'd buy a new one when she got to the resort. It wasn't really lying, she told herself. If she ever did get to the resort, she would want a new suit, because the daring little bikini she'd bought with Spence's enjoyment in mind hardly seemed inviting now.

And on Friday, when the weather forecast for the weekend began to look threatening, she explained to Charlotte that she didn't want to take a chance of missing her connections, and reminded her that the little commuter airline out of Hammond's Point sometimes didn't get off the ground at all if it snowed. She would drive the few hours to the Minneapolis airport, she announced, stay overnight at a nearby hotel and leave her car in the long-term parking lot.

Charlotte didn't utter a word of protest. Perhaps, Sharley thought, she realized how unbearable things had become.

The city limits were no sooner behind her than Sharley started to feel better. It was a three-hour drive up to the cabin, along a winding highway that was beautiful even at this bleak season of the year. She had tapes to listen to, and she had a comfortably full basket of snacks that Libby had pressed on her as she'd said goodbye.

And, Sharley thought, once she'd had a chance to sort out her feelings, perhaps it would turn out that her own company wasn't so bad. Of course she missed Spence. She had loved him, after all, and it wasn't easy to turn off those feelings and forget her dreams. Her life would feel empty for a while. But she'd get over it. Eventually.

By the time she reached the last little town, it was late afternoon, and the threat of a storm had grown to massive proportions. The sky was low and dark, and clouds rolled and tossed above her. Just as she pulled off the road at the small general store, a few raindrops hit the windshield with the force of falling rocks, and she shivered and hurried inside.

The proprietor, a plump little middle-aged woman, eyed Sharley warily. "What brings you up here in this kind of weather, Miss Collins?"

"Well, the natives don't mind it, do they, Mrs. Harper?"

The woman sniffed. "Depends on which natives you're talking about. Some of us would rather be in Texas. You aren't going to stay in that old cabin, are you?"

Sharley shrugged. "Why not? It's got everything I'll need. That reminds me, may I use your telephone? This was a last-minute idea, so I haven't called the caretaker to turn the heat on."

The proprietor pushed the telephone across the counter.

Sharley fiddled with the buttons and added, "Actually, I forgot to ask Uncle Martin who's taking care of the place now. Do you know?"

"Still Joe Baxter, I guess. It makes sense, with him living just a mile away. Otherwise somebody would have to go all the way out there from town just to keep an eye on the place."

There was no answer at the Baxters' number, and Sharley frowned. She could manage by herself, she supposed, but she wasn't looking forward to struggling with the connections from the big old heating stove to the propane tank that fueled it. Besides, what about the water? It must have been turned off and the pipes drained for the winter. And who knew what other essential things she might overlook without help? Was the electricity even turned on?

Maybe, Sharley thought, this hadn't been such a bright idea.

Mrs. Harper had one eye on the front window, where raindrops battered the glass. "Are you sure you want to go all the way out there?"

Sharley nodded.

Mrs. Harper looked doubtful. "Well, then, you'd better get your supplies gathered up and get back on the road before it gets nasty. You've still got fifteen miles to drive, and the weather isn't going to get any better. I'll get on the CB and find Joe and send him over as quick as I can."

"Thanks," Sharley said with heartfelt relief. "You're a dear, Mrs. Harper."

After she left the town, the road was mostly gravel, and Sharley took it slowly, cautious of the rocks rattling under her car. The wind was coming up, gusting so strongly at times that the car swayed under its force; sheets of rain interfered with her vision and made it difficult to recognize the route. Her nerves were stretched to the limit by the time she reached the tiny track of a driveway, and when she pulled in beside the cabin she sat still for a moment, happy just to be off the road.

She studied the direction of the falling rain and decided to maneuver the car around to the back of the cabin, where she would be a bit more sheltered as she unloaded.

She left everything in the car and went to open the door. Her key turned slowly and hesitantly in the lock, as if it hadn't been used in a long time, and she braced herself. Just how long had it been since Martin had come up here? Last autumn, Charlotte had been so ill he hadn't gone anywhere at all....

The cabin smelled a bit musty, but it was warm. Sharley was startled; she held her hands over the propane stove before she let herself believe it was really running.

"Bless you, Mrs. Harper, you efficient soul," Snarley said aloud. "You're a miracle worker." Citizens band or no, how had she managed to find Joe so quickly?

The big room was dim, and night was ruthlessly closing in by the time Sharley finished unloading her car. It took six trips, and by the time she'd finished carrying in the boxes, she was regretting buying so many supplies. How much food could one person eat in a week, anyway?

Besides, the cabin was already better supplied than she'd expected. "Probably from the last time Martin was here," she mused, studying the canned goods on the shelves in the tiny kitchenette, which was tucked in the corner of the cabin's main room. How long did cans keep food safe, anyway?

There was also a generous stack of firewood on the small back porch, where it was dry. Thank heaven, she thought. The rain had turned to sleet now, so she certainly wouldn't have wanted to go out looking for the main woodpile.

She built a fire, and once it was roaring cheerfully she fixed herself a salad and an omelet, and ate her meal with her feet propped on the coffee table and her plate balanced in her lap. The food was the first that had tasted good in a week. She thought once about the beef Wellington she should have been eating tonight at the rehearsal dinner, and then firmly put the thought out of her mind.

She was too exhausted to read and too relaxed to get up and look for something to occupy herself. It was enough of a relief not to have to keep her guard up and to know she might not even have to see or talk to a single soul for an entire week.

"What a blessing," she muttered, and congratulated herself on a grand idea. She stared at the flames, almost hypnotized by the flickering light and the gentle hiss of the logs, until the fire died down. Then she put the screen carefully in place and went off to bed.

There were two bedrooms at the back of the cabin, with a tiny, compact bath tucked between them. Sharley chose the little room she'd always used. Neither room was large or elegant, and it was comforting to be back in childhood surroundings.

The air in the bedroom was still chilly, for the stove in the main room was the only source of heat in the cabin. "You could call it crisp, as a matter of fact," she told herself as she dug a pair of pajamas out of her suitcase. Her teeth were almost chattering, and she left the door open and piled blankets on the bed.

Because she was so cold, sleep was long in coming, and she couldn't help thinking of how she should have been spending this night. It should have been the last in her old room at the Hudson house. She probably would have been equally restless, looking forward to putting on that beautiful satin-and-lace gown....

She had forgotten all about her gown. It was still at the dressmaker's, where it had been waiting for her final fitting. Not that it mattered, of course; the bill had been paid long since. And what would she do with it, anyway? Hang it in the attic and make pilgrimages once a year on what would have been her wedding anniversary?

Where had she gone so wrong? Sharley had always considered herself to be a good judge of character; she certainly didn't have any trouble sizing up a classroom and knowing who the troublemakers were going to be. So why hadn't she seen Spence's flaws? It was true she hadn't dated him for long—it had seemed so obvious that they knew all they needed to about each other!—but surely in the couple of short months of their engagement there should have been signs of trouble to come. But she had not seen.

She shifted uneasily, and icy air licked around her body. She settled back into a little lump in the middle of the bed and considered.

She had always known Spence, or at least known who he was—he was four years older than Sharley, but in a town the size of Hammond's Point, everyone knew everyone. That was particularly true of Spence, since there was no one in town who didn't know about his father—John Greenfield, the trusted and respected stockbroker who had turned out to be not so trustworthy or respectable. John Greenfield who, as the investigation closed around him and prosecution had become a certainty, had bought a piece of garden hose and taken his car out onto a lonely back road and inhaled carbon monoxide, calling a halt to everything.

Yes, everyone in Hammond's Point knew who Spence Greenfield was.

And any woman with sense, Sharley told herself as she turned restlessly under the mound of blankets, would have wondered if Spence might be just a little like his father, after all.

But no matter how hard she searched her memory, there was nothing—no hint of dishonesty or duplicity, no reason to doubt him.

Of course that was how his father had managed to pull off his scams for so long, too, Sharley reminded herself. Because he seemed so honest and so upstanding and so reliable.

But if Spence was like his father, why had he stayed in Hammond's Point at all? Why hadn't he started over in some other place, where his name was not infamous?

It had never occurred to Sharley before to ask that question. She had simply been glad that he had stayed—not for herself at first, but because she was happy that Martin had found such a good second-in-command.

She had hardly known Spence until that time; since he was older and she had gone out of town to college, there had been few occasions for them to meet. But once he was working for Hudson Products she saw him regularly—at the office when she went in to see Martin, at the house when he came for dinner or stopped by with paperwork or paychecks to be signed. She found him likable, and always interesting. But she didn't really know when she'd started noticing him as a man—a very attractive, very handsome, very sexy man—and wishing he would notice her as a woman, not just as Martin Hudson's niece. Sometime that autumn, she supposed, though she hadn't known it herself until early December, on the night of the Hudson Products Christmas party.

Charlotte had not yet been fully recuperated from her bout of pneumonia in the fall, but she'd insisted on making an appearance at the party. Neither Martin nor Sharley thought she was up to it, and so they were not surprised when she grew tired midway through the evening. "It's a damned shame to drag you away, too," Martin said when he found Sharley on the dance floor to tell her they had to go home. "But Charlotte's exhausted, and if she tries to carry on, she'll be back in the hospital next week."

Sharley had immediately excused herself to her dance partner. But she had taken just a couple of steps toward the cloakroom when Spence intervened. "Does Mrs. Hudson really need Sharley's attention, too?" he asked mildly.

Martin seemed startled. "No, I don't suppose so. But—"

"Then I'll see that Sharley gets home safely."

Sharley turned to him in astonishment. She was perfectly capable of getting herself home, if it came to that; she didn't have her car, but she had a multitude of friends, and Hammond's Point had a taxi service. Still, it was thoughtful of him to offer. "That's very kind of you," she began.

"It's no trouble. It's not at all out of my way."

The dismissive remark stung a bit, and before Sharley stopped to think about it she said tartly, "And if it was a thousand miles?"

He looked down at her for one ages-long moment and said quietly, "Then I'd happily do it, anyway. And not for your uncle's sake, either."

There was something in those dark gray eyes, so suddenly sober and serious as he looked down at her, that made Sharley want to gasp for breath. If he put into words what his eyes were saying...

But all he said was, "Will you dance with me?"

And that was how it had started—with a dance and a look—and an evening that had been plain as punch suddenly turned to champagne, full of breathless bubbles. By the time the party ended and Spence took her home, Sharley knew that this was what she had been waiting for all autumn.

He had walked her to the front door and unlocked it for her, then gave her back her key. But though she put her hand on the knob, she didn't turn it. Was it only she who had felt the special zest in the air tonight? He had made no move to kiss her, or even to hold her hand as they walked to the house. This might be the only evening she would share with him, and she did not want it to end. But how long could she stand there, hoping?

"May I see you again?" he asked.

Sharley was afraid to let herself think he really meant it. He might have felt he had to say something just to break the silence, and the words had been ordinary enough.

"I should say you could hardly avoid it under the circumstances," she said lightly.

"That's not what I meant, Sharley."

There was something about the way he said her name. "I'd like that," she whispered. And then she had surprised even herself, for that was when she had brushed her lips against the cleft in his chin and been stunned by the hungry way he had kissed her in return.

It had started as simply as that. Within days, they became a subject for comment in the town. Within a week, they were spending almost every evening together.

And on New Year's Eve, as they drank champagne at the country club, he kissed her and said with an odd note of tension in his voice, "I'm a fool, I suppose, even to show you this, but..." He pulled a tiny velvet box from his pocket.

Sharley's eyes widened in shock as the full-carat diamond caught the romantically dimmed light of the nearest chandelier and fractured it into dancing rainbows.

Spence snapped the box shut and said uneasily, "I don't mean to pressure you. I just hope that someday you'll want to wear that, and so..." He ran a hand through his hair. "Stupid of me. Forget it."

She'd reached for his hand blindly, through tears of happiness, and whispered, "But I don't want to forget it, Spence. Oh, yes, I'll marry you...."

It's funny, Sharley thought, that only now do I realize that he never really proposed to me at all.

She stirred restlessly in the cold bed. Suddenly she didn't mind the brush of the blankets, still frigid where her body had not yet warmed them, for the pain in her heart was worse.

She had accepted a proposal of marriage that had never actually been made. All Spence had really done was tell her that someday he might propose, but she had answered a question that hadn't been asked, and seized an offer that hadn't been made. He hadn't seemed unhappy about it, she reminded herself. Still, what was the poor guy supposed to do? Tell the boss's niece he hadn't meant it quite that way, after all?

She pulled a pillow over her head. It didn't help hide her humiliation. Had he felt trapped? And if so, had he wanted—subconsciously, at least—to be caught that day in the gardener's cottage? Had he wanted to get out before it was too late?

Sharley hadn't thought of that scenario before, and it made her feel slightly sick, because it was the only explanation she could find that made any sense at all. Why *had* he taken Wendy to the house, anyway? She'd asked herself that question a thousand times. Why hadn't he had the good sense to take the girl to a hotel or to his apartment, instead of the gardener's cottage—the home he was to share with his bride? He must have known Sharley was likely to stop by....

She dozed off finally, but hers was a restless sleep, disturbed by the pounding of sleet against the tin roof. Once during the night she even thought she heard a door bang. But that couldn't be; she had checked all the locks. It must have been a branch breaking and falling against the side of the cabin. In any case, she was too exhausted and the cabin too cold to go looking for strange things that happened to go bump in the night.

By morning the worst of the storm had passed, but the sky was still dark gray and dismal. Sharley reluctantly pulled herself out of bed. The main room would be warmer, she told herself. She would hurry into her clothes ... or perhaps she wouldn't bother. She tugged a heavy terry-cloth robe out of her suitcase and shoved her feet into furry slippers. She'd get warm first, she decided, and then she'd brave getting dressed.

The main room was warmer, but not by much. The remnants of her fire were cold and gray. She should probably have stayed up till the fire died completely so she could close the damper. No doubt that was where all the heat had gone—straight up the chimney. Besides, the propane stove sounded funny; it was making an odd little whistling noise.

No, not a whistle, she realized, but a snore. And it wasn't coming from the stove, but from the couch nearby.

A snore meant a person. No doubt, she told herself, it was a traveler who'd gotten caught in the storm, stumbled across the cabin and assumed it was empty. Perhaps that noise she'd heard in the night had been a window breaking; a missing pane would certainly account for the temperature in here this morning. But what sort of traveler would have been out in that storm last night, seeking shelter in a deserted cabin miles from anywhere? A homeless person? A criminal on the run?

She tiptoed across the room and peered over the back of the couch at her unexpected visitor. She was holding her breath and she was poised to flee. It was her only option....

He was stretched out on his side, with one arm thrown above his head and a bright-colored Indian blanket pulled up to his chin. The blanket was too short, and a full twelve inches of his legs stuck out the bottom of it. He hadn't bothered to take off his shoes. His dark hair was tousled as if it had been soaked and then allowed to dry naturally. His eyelashes lay heavily against his cheekbones, which were slightly flushed.

Sharley blinked and looked again, and her stomach felt as if it was turning a very slow double somersault. No, her mind wasn't playing tricks. The man who lay on her couch, so peacefully and soundly asleep, really was Spence Greenfield.

CHAPTER FOUR

SPENCE SEEMED TO SENSE her presence, for he awoke with a start. In fact, he moved so fast, pushing the blanket away and leaping to his feet, that Sharley took two steps back in pure astonishment. The movement caught his eye, and he wheeled around to face her.

For all of ten seconds they simply stared at each other.

If Sharley didn't know better, she'd have sworn that some cosmic force, in a diabolical fit of humor, had swept away the elegantly tailored Spence Greenfield she knew and put a changeling in his place.

He looked haggard, she thought. His flannel shirt and jeans were rumpled. There was a long red crease across one cheek where his face had rested against a seam in the upholstery; it slashed like a scar through the dark stubble of a day-old beard.

Of course, Sharley had to admit, she must not look like her usual self, either. She hadn't bothered to comb her hair, and it was probably standing on end. Her terry robe was warm and practical, but it was a far cry from the little satin-and-lace number she'd planned to take on her honeymoon. And he'd never seen her before without lipstick and eye shadow, any more than she'd seen him with the careless beginnings of a beard.

Spence opened his mouth as if to comment on her appearance and sneezed, instead.

The sound startled Sharley back to reality. She dug her hands deep into the pockets of her robe and said stiffly, "What in heaven's name are you doing here?"

Spence's jaw tightened. "Well, I certainly didn't come up to see you, if that's what you're implying."

"Oh?"

"Hell, no. The entire town thought you were going to the Bahamas. If I'd wanted to run into you, this is the last place I'd have gone." He sat down on the couch again with his head in his hands and uttered a succinct phrase that would have made Charlotte Hudson threaten to wash his mouth out with soap.

Sharley said curtly, "That expresses my sentiments exactly." She moved around the couch to face him. "Since we're obviously agreed we don't want to both be here, one of us is going to have to go. I was here first, so you'll have to leave."

Spence shook his head, but there was no defiance in the gesture, no angry challenge. "Not in this mess."

"What do you mean?"

"Have you looked outside?"

Sharley glanced at the window. She couldn't see through it, and at first, she actually wondered if Martin had had the panes replaced with security glass, the kind with an embossed pattern that admitted light but prevented window-peeking. Then she realized there was nothing wrong with the glass except for a solid coating of ice on the outside of it. Raindrops had hit the pane and frozen as they ran down it, creating layer upon layer of ice in an intricate design.

Unwilling to believe her eyes, she tugged the front door open. The wind whipped around her, searing her lungs; the cold seemed to munch at her fingertips, and the foot she'd set on the porch threatened to slide out from under her.

Despite the protection of the overhanging roof, the floor was coated with a full inch of ice.

She grabbed the doorjamb and dragged herself back into the cabin.

"I made it within a mile before the car went into the ditch," Spence said. "At least I thought I was within a mile. So..."

Sharley was leaning against the door, shivering. "So you *walked?* That's stupid, Spence. Don't you know you're supposed to stay in your car in a storm?"

"Of course I know that," he said irritably. "But I also knew that no one would start looking for me anytime soon, so if I wasn't going to be sitting in that car next week, frozen stiff, I had to get myself out of the situation."

She could see the sense in that. Still, the idea of that walk in the dark, in a storm, sent shudders through her.

"By the time I got here I was pretty well frozen, so I sat down by the stove to thaw out, and I guess I went to sleep."

"Didn't you wonder why it was warm?" Sharley pushed herself away from the door and went to stand beside the stove. "Or was your brain too frozen for that sort of logic?"

"Of course I didn't wonder. Martin called the handyman to have him open the place up for me."

Sharley swallowed hard. So that was why the cabin had been warm when she arrived. Mrs. Harper hadn't done wonders in finding Joe Baxter, after all.

Spence sneezed again.

"You've caught cold," Sharley said dully.

He sniffed and dragged a handkerchief from his pocket. "Congratulations, Sherlock."

"You don't need to be sarcastic. You deserve it, getting wet and not even bothering to dry off." She backed a little closer to the stove and glanced around the room. On the floor at the end of the couch was a duffel bag she didn't recognize. That was the only evidence of his presence—that and Spence himself, of course.

His third sneeze sounded as if his head was about to come off. No doubt it felt that way, too, Sharley thought, from the way he groaned and sagged down onto the couch.

She sighed. "I'll make you some tea."

"Nobody asked you to play nursemaid," he said thickly.

She didn't even bother to answer.

The lights in the kitchen weren't working. She shouldn't have been surprised; with at least an inch of ice coating the wires, something was bound to give. But at least the range was propane-powered, and in a few minutes the kettle was whistling. It was a cheerful sound.

That figured, Sharley reflected. Only an inanimate object could possibly register any humor in this situation.

Spence's eyes were closed when she returned to the main room, but he roused himself as she pulled up a small table beside him. He eyed the tray she set down. It contained two steaming mugs of tea and a tall glass of orange juice, but his gaze focused instead on the foil-wrapped tablet that lay at the edge of the tray.

"Decongestant," Sharley said briefly, sitting down in a nearby chair. "I tucked a couple in my purse last month when Charlotte had that awful cold, and I forgot to put them back in the medicine cabinet."

Spence reached for the tablet and the glass of juice. "I take it back. You're not a nursemaid, you're an angel."

The gratitude in his voice caught at her vocal cords, and she had to clear her throat before she could say, "Don't get excited. I've just got two of them, and each one is only good for twelve hours."

Spence swallowed the tablet. "So I'll count my blessings and not worry about tomorrow."

He looked as if his throat hurt, too, Sharley thought. That fact, plus his careless attitude, combined to make her feel a little angry. "On the other hand," she said coolly, "for all you know that pill could really be cyanide."

He smiled a little. "In that case, you'd have given me both of them." He settled back into the couch with the tea mug cradled between his hands, closed his eyes and said, "Why didn't I see your car last night?"

"It's around back."

He nodded. "I just stumbled in the front door. Any chance of getting your car out?"

Sharley shrugged. "If you put yours in the ditch, why do you think mine would fare any better?"

"It's daylight, at least."

"So what? We'd have a great view as we slid off the road. How badly was your car damaged?"

Spence didn't open his eyes. "I didn't stick around to inspect the fenders. But I don't think touch-up paint will take care of it."

That reminded Sharley of the other things he'd been buying at the hardware store. "You didn't happen to bring those candles with you, did you?"

"Yes. Don't tell me the power's out, too."

Sharley shifted in her chair and pulled her feet up under her. "Is Joe likely to be checking on you? Bringing supplies or anything?"

"The caretaker? In this weather? You must be kidding. If we can't get out—"

"He's probably got a tractor. Maybe even one of those all-terrain vehicles."

Spence rubbed the bridge of his nose. "Martin told him I didn't want to be disturbed. So I suppose he stocked up the kitchen and the firewood as ordered, and I won't catch a glimpse of him all week."

Sharley sighed. "Damn. I didn't even talk to him, just left word with the woman at the store in town, but since he'd already done what I asked, he probably won't worry about me either."

"And since he knows that both of us are here..." Spence shook his head ruefully. "I don't think he's likely to bother us."

She wanted to groan. Of course he was right; Joe Baxter would assume this was a lovers' tryst and keep his distance. "Joe's house is only a mile east of here. We could..."

Spence opened his eyes slowly. "That's how far I walked last night, and look at me."

"It's not raining now."

"The temperature dropped like a rock overnight, Sharley. We'd freeze before we got over the first hill. We'll just have to put up with each other for a day or two, that's all."

Sharley chewed on her lower lip. Put up with each other. She'd bet it sounded easier than it was.

"Besides, this can't last forever." His voice was slow and flat, and within seconds he appeared to be asleep.

Rest was probably the best thing for him, she thought. He looked exhausted. A mile-long trek through freezing rain. He was lucky he'd found his way to the cabin at all. In the storm, in unfamiliar country, it would have been easy to miss.

Well, he hadn't missed it, she reminded herself. So there was no sense in having panic attacks about what could have happened.

She uncurled herself from her chair. She'd get dressed and bring in some firewood, and then she'd rummage around for something to eat.

She didn't think she'd made a sound, but Spence said, without stirring or opening his eyes, "Thanks, Sharley."

"It's all right." She took two steps toward her bedroom and added awkwardly, "I'm sorry you have me to contend with, instead of Wendy."

He grunted a little as if in agreement, but didn't answer.

He'd said something earlier about not wanting to be disturbed, Sharley thought. Was it possible he'd planned to meet Wendy here?

Of course if that was the case, she couldn't imagine Martin making arrangements for him to use this cozy little retreat. And if that *had* been Spence's plan, why hadn't Wendy simply come with him? But perhaps Martin didn't know.

"Were you expecting her to join you?" she asked. "Before the storm hit, I mean."

"No." The single syllable was crisp and clipped.

Sharley tried not to let herself feel relief. It had been a silly thought, anyway, she told herself. As a matter of fact, she'd been verging on paranoia. But something wouldn't let her stop. "Why did you come up here, Spence?"

For a moment she thought he wasn't going to answer at all. "To think," he said finally.

"Oh." That was no answer and she knew she should leave well enough alone—but she couldn't. "If I only understood what she means to you, Spence..."

"Nothing, dammit." His voice held the barest trace of annoyance.

Nothing? He had caused this entire uproar in both their lives over a woman who meant nothing to him? Sharley didn't know whether she felt sad about that or sick at heart, or a little of both. How very trapped he must have felt, with his wedding day approaching, to go to such an extreme to put a stop to it!

"In that case," she said slowly, "I feel worse than ever."

SPENCE WAS ASLEEP AGAIN when she came out of her bedroom, dressed in jeans and two layers of sweaters. Part of her had wanted to crawl back under the covers and stay there all day where she wouldn't have to face him. But the chill of the bedroom weighed even more heavily on her.

She peeked over the back of the couch just as he released another long, rumbling breath. She shook her head a little. It wasn't such a bad snore, nothing like the buzz-saw sound of legend. It was kind of cute, actually, almost as if he was purring.

Still, there ought to be a law, she reflected. Anybody who snored ought to be required to disclose the fact to a prospective mate. Of course, she reminded herself, it was certainly no concern of hers anymore whether Spence snored or not.

The flush along his cheekbones had grown a little stronger, a little more hectic, and she bit her lip in concern. Was he running a fever? And if he was, what on earth was she to do about it?

Cautiously and very slowly she let the back of her hand brush his forehead.

Spence jerked to one side and his eyes flew open.

For an instant, she thought she caught the same look that she had often seen right before he kissed her—not the light and playful kisses, but the long, intense and hungry ones. And she reacted the same way, too, her insides suddenly feeling as slithery as lemon pudding on a hot afternoon.

Sharley turned beet red. Didn't she have any more control over herself than that? "Gracious, you're jumpy," she accused. "I was only checking to see if you're running a fever."

He stared up at her. "And the verdict?"

"I'm not sure," she said honestly. "You don't feel especially warm, but maybe my hands are colder than normal."

A gleam of irony appeared in Spence's eyes, and one dark eyebrow quirked upward.

Sharley put her chin up a little. He could think what he liked, she told herself. If he was so conceited that he thought she would seize any excuse for touching him...

Don't be an idiot, she told herself. Of course he wasn't thinking anything of the sort. And the brooding, hungry look must have been her imagination, too. Even if it had been real, it didn't mean anything; physical attraction wasn't always associated with love and respect.

Spence sat up. "I'd kill for a hot shower," he mused. "How's the water supply? Or did that go out along with the electricity?"

"No, it's all right for a while at least. There's a cistern for storage, and the water heater burns propane, too. I wouldn't drink the stuff, though, because it may not be very fresh."

"Fair enough. I won't drink it, I'll just drown myself in it." He picked up the duffel bag. "Which bedroom?"

"I've got the one on the right."

She didn't watch him cross the room. Separate bedrooms, she was thinking. On what should have been their wedding day.

Not that I have any desire to change that now, she told herself firmly.

She inspected the contents of the dark, silent refrigerator before deciding on her menu. By the time Spence reappeared, she was arranging strips of Swiss cheese atop two picture-perfect sandwiches, and though her fingers trembled slightly as he came up beside her she did not look up.

"Is that crab salad?" he asked, obviously impressed.

Sharley nodded and put the sandwiches under the broiler. "Don't get any ideas. Without electricity, I have to either use the crab, put it outside where it'll freeze and be ruined, or throw it away right now, so..."

He smiled a little. "So you chose to throw part of it away on me. Thanks, Sharley. You're a good sport, you know."

Why that careless accolade should bring tears to her eyes when she had gone through so much without crying was more than Sharley could understand. But she was darned if she'd let him see her cry. She stirred the pot of beef noodle soup and ladled a serving into a mug. "Here. You can start with this. Watch out, though, it's hot."

Spence sniffed and said, "What? Not chicken soup? I'm disappointed in you."

Sharley glared at him and caught the shimmer of mischief in his eyes. But the expression died even as she watched him. His gaze was fixed on her mouth.

Because it's trembling, she told herself. Not because he wants to kiss me.

"Sorry," Spence said. "I only meant to lighten things up a bit." There was an awkward edge to his voice.

Sharley hardly heard him. She realized suddenly that she'd been expecting his shower and change of clothes to turn him back into the Spence she had known before. But of course that hadn't happened, though he did look much better than he had earlier in the morning. He was wearing a fresh flannel shirt, in a bright red-and-blue plaid that made his eyes look like blue steel. His hair had dried in little ringlets, not at all like his usual smooth style. And the beard stubble was still there....

She poured a cup of soup for herself. "Are you making a point with the beard?" she asked. "Competing for woodsman of the year or something?"

"Oh, no. It's just that I only brought an electric razor." He rubbed a hand idly across his jaw as if it itched and glanced at the oven door behind her. "I don't like to be a pest, Sharley, but that crab salad looked good, and I'd hate to have it turn into a cinder."

She rescued the sandwiches just as the melting cheese began to brown, and thanked heaven that the broiler's heat would account for her flushed cheeks. Standing there staring at him like a calf—what was wrong with her, anyway? It wasn't as if she'd never seen the man before!

Spence took a couple of plates from the bottom of a stack in the cabinet, eyed them warily and wiped them off with a towel. "That should be sanitary enough," he said.

"Especially since I just finished washing them." Sharley slid a sandwich onto his plate. "Taco chips?"

Spence shook his head. "All the comforts of home," he mused. He sat down at the tiny table and picked up his sandwich.

And what exactly did he mean by that? Sharley wondered. A cozy retreat and a little woman to take care of him—and no complications? The statement made the backs of her eyelids prickle uncomfortably. "I suppose you mean everything will be great as long as the decongestant holds out and I don't get tired of cooking."

A tiny frown tugged at Spence's brow. "I didn't ask to be waited on, Sharley."

His voice was even and reasonable, and she had to admit the truth of what he'd said. Still, she felt a bit disgruntled. "Don't plan on it continuing," she warned.

"I'm not. But neither am I going to race you to see who can do something first." He put the sandwich down and looked thoughtfully at her. "The problem with you is that you're so accustomed to fulfilling Charlotte's every whim that you don't even wait to be asked."

"If I wanted a dissection of my character flaws, Spence—"

He ignored the interruption. "You just go straight ahead and do whatever you think needs to be done, and then you expect to be applauded for your kindness. That's the part that amazes me, you know. Charlotte never seems to appreciate what you do, so why should you expect anyone else to notice?"

"Dammit, Spence—"

"Don't misunderstand me. I don't mean that your good works aren't worth doing, at least some of the time. I certainly don't mean that I don't appreciate lunch." He waved a hand at his plate. "It's just that sometimes Lady Bountiful is a bit hard to live up to."

Sharley stared at him for an endless moment. "You know something, Spence?" she said gently. "I'm beginning to be glad that we're stuck up here in the woods."

"Oh?" He sounded wary.

"A couple of days of this and I'll be absolutely delighted you didn't have an explanation for your little episode with Wendy. Because if you had, I might have actually forgiven you!" She slammed her mug down on the table so hard that noodles slopped over the rim.

Spence didn't even flinch. "You can't stand the idea that you might not be perfect, can you?"

"Me? Perfect? You've got a nerve. Your judgment stinks, you know that, Spence? After what you've done, why in the hell you think you have a right to criticize me..." Words failed her. What was the point, anyway? He'd never understand what she meant.

Her sandwich untouched, she stormed across to the far corner of the main room, as far as she could get from him without retreating to her bedroom, and flung herself down in a chair with her back to him.

Silence descended, except for the steady whoosh of propane burning in the stove and the uneven whistling of wind around the cabin.

It was almost a quarter of an hour later that Sharley heard the back door creak open, and she came up out of her chair with a jolt. No matter what sort of a fight they'd had, she could not allow him to set out on that mile-long walk to the Baxters' house. He didn't know exactly where it was, and with his cold and the decongestant she'd given him just taking effect...

But neither was it up to her to interfere, she thought. If he was idiot enough to go out in his condition, it wasn't her place to try to stop him. He was right about that; she was neither his nursemaid nor his servant—and she wasn't his boss, either.

The door scraped again and Spence reappeared, his arms full of firewood. He kicked the door shut and carried the logs to the fireplace.

Sharley couldn't decide whether to scold him for not putting on his coat or tell him she was glad he hadn't gone farther. So she bit her tongue and did neither.

He knelt beside the hearth and patiently built the fire. Even on the back porch, the wood hadn't been completely protected from the driving sleet, and the wet logs stubbornly resisted the flame. It was quite a time before Spence had coaxed a pleasant little blaze into life.

When he finally turned away from the fireplace, he did not go back to the couch as Sharley had half expected, but came to sit on the arm of her chair.

She leaned away from him as far as she could, but still the warmth and the scent of smoke mixing with his cologne tugged at her senses.

Spence didn't look at her. His arms were crossed, his feet propped wide to maintain his balance, and he was staring into the fire. "I'm sorry. I had no right to criticize you. It's not my business how you deal with Charlotte."

"It's certainly not," Sharley said stiffly.

Spence sighed. "Look, Sharley, Hammond's Point is a small town. We have to be able to face each other. This kind of venom isn't going to make it any easier."

"You're right. Of course, maybe you should have thought of that before you flaunted Wendy at the scholarship fund-raiser."

He said something under his breath that Sharley didn't catch. Before she could ask what it was, he had gone on. "I'm sorry. That particular decision wasn't very well thought out."

Sharley waited for more, but he didn't seem inclined to continue. Finally she said, "Is this another of your feeble attempts at explaining?"

"No. There doesn't seem to be any point in trying to explain."

"Not at the rate you're going, no."

Spence's mouth tightened. "In any case," he pointed out, "now that you've returned my ring, I don't owe you any explanation."

Sharley couldn't argue with that.

"I just think we should try to be civil to each other, that's all."

Civil, Sharley thought. If things had been different, she would have been walking down the aisle round about now, a brilliant-eyed bride going to meet the man to whom she would pledge her life. She wondered if Spence had noticed the time, too, and if he had seen the irony. How very far down they had come—from the promise of lifelong love and companionship to a last-ditch attempt at being civil to each other!

All things considered, it certainly wasn't any wonder that tempers were running short today. With the kind of stress they were both feeling, it was a wonder something hadn't exploded before now.

Spence was right, though, Sharley concluded. Hammond's Point was very small, and the more visible and vehement their feelings for each other were, the more people were likely to comment and the longer the whole sad story would be kept alive. If they couldn't actually reach some kind of peaceful settlement, which seemed unlikely, then their only real alternative was to pretend they had.

She shifted uneasily in her chair, not quite able to put her feelings into words.

But Spence seemed to know what she was thinking. "It's worth a try, isn't it?"

She managed a nod, and Spence gave her a crooked half smile. Sharley's heart jolted. It wasn't fair, she thought. The man was as unpredictable as static electricity, and just as unsettling.

He pushed himself to his feet. "Is there anything to do around here? A deck of cards or a game or something?"

If he thinks he's going to talk me into playing poker with him, Sharley thought, he's a fool. I'll try to be civil, but I'm not going to be pals! I couldn't take that.

"In that cabinet, I think," she said, carelessly waving a hand toward a small stand in the corner. "I'm going to get a book."

He nodded as if it didn't matter in the least to him and started to dig through the drawers.

Sharley paused at her bedroom door as he exclaimed in satisfaction, and turned around to see him holding up a ragged box. She'd never seen anyone get so excited over a jigsaw puzzle. "What *did* you plan to do with yourself all week?" she asked tartly.

"There's a briefcase full of paperwork still in my car."

"What a vacation," she muttered, and couldn't help wondering whether he'd have taken that briefcase to the Bahamas, too.

When she came back to the living room with her book, he was whistling as he sorted out the straight-edged pieces of the puzzle and arranged them by color on the coffee table. Sharley took a pillow from the couch and settled down on the thick rug in front of the fire to read.

But her novel wasn't as interesting as it had looked on the bookstore shelf, and Spence's tuneless whistle was driving her mad. She pushed the book aside and stared at the flames, trying to decide how to ask him, civilly, to shut up. Before she'd found a way, her eyelids had grown so heavy she decided to rest for a minute first. She pulled off her reading glasses and put her head down.

The room was almost dark when she awoke, and the bright blanket was tucked so firmly around her body that for an instant she thought she'd been wrapped in a strait-jacket. She pushed it back and sat up, rubbing her eyes.

Spence had lighted a couple of candles and propped them on the corners of the coffee table, and he was holding up a piece of the jigsaw puzzle and squinting at it.

"You'll ruin your eyes doing that in the dark," Sharley said. At least, that was what she tried to say; she yawned in the middle of her sentence.

Spence seemed to understand, anyway, for he looked up and smiled. "Are you hungry?"

"Sort of," she admitted. She was ravenous, to tell the truth; her uneaten crab-salad sandwich was haunting her thoughts. But she wasn't about to tell Spence that.

She tried to remember what was still in the refrigerator. The eggs would have to be used soon, since they'd freeze if she put them outside with the rest of the perishables....

"Well, I certainly am. You've been asleep forever." He snapped in a piece and reached for another one. "Since we can't phone for pizza delivery, I thought I'd make beef stew and biscuits. Stew from a can, of course, but I do great biscuits from scratch."

Sharley nodded slowly. "That sounds good." The offer made her feel warmer somehow.

Spence put the puzzle piece down and headed for the kitchen.

Sharley stretched, trying to work some of the stiffness out of her muscles. Going to sleep on the floor hadn't been the brightest idea of her life. She put another log on the fire and sat down on the couch. The cushions were still warm from his body, and they sagged comfortably, cradling her close.

In the flickering light of the candles, she picked up an interesting-looking piece and studied the puzzle. It was more than half-finished, and the pattern was becoming apparent—a complicated view of a row of brightly painted and intricately detailed Victorian houses. The piece she held was part of a delicate rose window. That shouldn't be hard to find, she thought.

Still, it was several minutes before she put the piece in place and patted it triumphantly.

"You'll ruin your eyes doing that in the dark."

The voice was like an echo, and Sharley jumped; she hadn't heard Spence crossing the room till he stood above her. He'd wrapped a dish towel around his waist like an apron; it emphasized his narrow hips and made him look even taller.

"That rule only applies to you," she said mildly. "I'll show you what a real puzzle-worker can do."

"Oh, you're going to play that game, are you?" Spence scooped up the candles.

"That's not fair! If you take away the candles—"

"If I don't," he warned, "you may find yourself eating the strangest biscuits in the history of the world, because I can't see what I'm putting in them."

With only the flickering light of the fire left, all the puzzle pieces took on a ghastly reddish tinge. Sharley gave a dramatic sigh.

Spence didn't sound sympathetic. "If you're looking for something constructive to do, you can come and stir the stew."

"I thought this meal was your turn." Nevertheless, she followed him to the kitchen.

"Are we taking turns? I thought we were cooperating."

The careless words tugged at her heart. She picked up the wooden spoon, intending to concentrate very hard on the stew.

Spence reached around her to get something from the cabinet above her head. The sleeve of his flannel shirt brushed softly against her hair, and he tensed as if he'd been burned.

The flickering candlelight cast strong shadows across his face, throwing cheekbones and eyelashes and the cleft in his chin into relief. If she turned just a little, she would be almost in his arms.

And then what? What would that prove?

Outside the kitchen window a branch cracked, unable to bear the weight of ice it held. It seemed to break the spell inside, as well. Spence moved away to mix the biscuits, and Sharley began to stir the stew, carefully scraping the bottom of the pan and trying to blink away the moisture in her eyes.

This should have been their wedding night.

Oh, Spence, she wanted to cry, *what happened to us? If only I understood!*

CHAPTER FIVE

BUT SHARLEY DIDN'T SAY IT, for she knew what Spence had told her was true; he didn't owe her an explanation anymore. She had given up the right to ask questions when she handed back his ring.

And breaking their engagement was still the only action she could have taken under the circumstances, she reminded herself. The fact was she'd given him every opportunity to explain, and he hadn't even tried. Why should she fool herself into thinking he would be any more capable of justifying himself now?

She turned down the heat under the stew and got plates out of the cabinet. The tightness in her chest returned as she began to set the tiny kitchen table, remembering the other times they'd shared a meal. Usually they were at a restaurant surrounded by people, or they were at the Hudson house, with Martin and Charlotte present; rarely had they been so completely alone. But there had been a couple of quiet dinners at Spence's apartment, and that impromptu winter picnic when they had found a corner of the park where no one had intruded. And now there was this simple meal, with candles on the table, on what should have been their wedding night, but wasn't.

She told herself fiercely that indulging in self-pity was a waste of time. Still, she had to swallow hard to get rid of the lump in her throat.

Spence was right about the quality of his biscuits. They were light and flaky and melt-in-the-mouth delicious, and as she ate her third one, Sharley told him so.

"I learned how to make them from my mother," he said as he buttered another one for himself.

"I'm sorry I never had a chance to meet her." Spence seldom mentioned his mother, who had died while he was still in high school. Would he talk about her now?

"We ate a lot of biscuits when I was a kid. It was a long time before I realized they not only tasted good, they were cheap." He tilted his head. "Listen."

From the intentness of his posture, Sharley expected the roar of a rescue plane at the very least, but in fact she couldn't hear a thing. Finally she gave up. "What am I supposed to listen to?"

"The wind," he said. "There isn't any."

He was right. The wind had whirled around the cabin so steadily all day that she had grown used to its whine. She'd known something had changed; she just hadn't identified it.

"Maybe that means there's a warm front coming in," Spence mused.

Perhaps it was only that the description was suggestive, but Sharley did feel warmer. "It's a whole lot cozier in here, isn't it?"

"As if the stove is having an easier time keeping up. The walls of this place must be like a sieve." He reached for the pot of stew on the stove and offered Sharley another serving.

She nodded absentmindedly and watched as he spooned the stew onto her plate. "Well, it was never really intended to be a winter resort."

"You know, I can't fathom the elegant Charlotte camping out here at all. The mere thought of it makes me want to laugh."

"Oh, she didn't. This is Martin's hideaway."

"Of course," Spence said crisply. "Now that I think about it, that's not surprising."

Sharley was impatient. "Look, Spence, I know you don't have much of an opinion of Charlotte, but you're not being fair to her. The stroke she had a few years ago, well, it made her a different person. She wasn't bitter before."

He put up a hand. "That's not what I meant, exactly. In any case, let's not fight about it tonight, all right?"

Sharley poked at her stew with the tines of her fork. "All right," she said unhappily. "But it's not Charlotte's fault, really. Strokes do that, sometimes—cause a personality shift. And no matter what, she's been awfully good to me. Taking me in the way she did—"

"She's your aunt, for heaven's sake! What else would you expect? And what would people have thought if she'd turned you away?"

"Well, it would have been quite understandable if she had. That was the year she had the stroke. No one guessed, as sick as Charlotte was, that it would be my mother who died first." She sighed. "At any rate, the last thing Charlotte needed was a loud and thoughtless teenager trampling all over her life."

Spence shook his head.

"What does that mean?"

"Not loud and thoughtless. Not you, Sharley. Not ever."

The tone of his voice—low, with an almost imperceptible tremor—caught at Sharley's heart. He sounded so sincere....

"Thank you," she managed. "I think."

Spence smiled, and the candlelight made his teeth gleam white and sent sparks dancing in his eyes. "Oh, I meant it."

He'd always had a beautiful smile. No, Sharley corrected, he had a whole inventory of them—ranging from a mischievously charming grin to a slow and sultry smile, which could make a girl's heart turn over in her chest....

Her breath was doing funny things, like sticking in her throat and making her lungs ache. She pushed her chair back. The sudden screech of the chair legs against the wood floor shattered the quiet intimacy of the moment.

"I'll clean up," she said briskly. "The biscuits really were wonderful, Spence."

He didn't protest. He helped to clear the table and then rebuilt the fire while she straightened up the kitchen.

But as Sharley washed the dishes, she found herself almost wishing that he'd said, "There's no hurry. Let's just sit here and talk for a while, instead...."

THE WIND DID NOT PICK UP again overnight. The silence outside would have made the little cabin seem even more isolated, Sharley suspected, had it not been for the tiny noises Spence made in the big room.

If it wasn't for the sheer discomfort of having him around, she told herself while she was in the shower on Sunday morning, I'd be almost glad he's here.

In fact, she found herself hurrying to get dressed, and not entirely because of the chill in her bedroom. She was concerned about Spence. His cold had seemed better at dinner last night; in fact, he hadn't sneezed even once through the whole evening. Yet he had been up for hours after she had gone to bed, and she knew, even though she hadn't been fully awake herself, he'd been moving around since early this morning. Was he feeling worse?

She was growling a little herself as she emerged from her room, rubbing her still-wet hair with a towel. At least the hot water was holding out so far, but how could she have managed to forget that a hair drier didn't work when there was nothing to power it? She'd no doubt have a head cold, too, by the time her hair stopped dripping.

"Sneaky stuff, electricity," she began. "It creeps into our lives so insidiously we don't even realize how much we rely on it till . . ."

Her gaze fell on Spence, who was working on the jig-saw puzzle again, and she caught her breath. Yesterday morning when she walked in on him, he had looked half-ill and entirely rumpled; nevertheless, he had still been appealing. Today his skin was back to its usual healthy color, and yesterday's untidy stubble was beginning to look like a genuine attempt to start a beard. Even the fright-fully bright red plaid pajamas, which peeked out from under his brown terry bathrobe, couldn't make him look less wonderful.

She felt her muscles tighten just a little in appreciation of the picture he made, and perhaps even in anticipation; it was as if her body still hadn't quite got the message from her brain that she wasn't supposed to react to him like this anymore.

Spence stopped tinkering with the puzzle and looked up. The beginnings of a scowl crossed his face, as if he found the way she was looking at him to be annoying.

That's torn it, Sharley thought. Dammit, she didn't even want the man, so why was she drooling over him like some star-struck adolescent? The last thing she needed was to give him the idea that she felt any regret.

"Maybe it would be a good thing if you got dressed," she snapped.

He turned a puzzle piece over and over, but he seemed to be considering her words, instead. "What's likely to happen if I don't?"

Sharley felt herself flush scarlet. It had sounded almost like a warning, she thought, as if she had told him to put on some clothes or expect to be attacked! "Nothing," she said crisply. "It's just not good taste to sit around in your pajamas."

He put the piece into place. "Don't nag, Sharley. Be grateful I have pajamas and a robe. If it hadn't been for Martin warning me about unheated bedrooms, I wouldn't have bothered."

That sent another flood of color over Sharley's face. She dropped to the floor in front of the fire and bent her head so her hair cascaded over her face. By the time it was dry, she figured, she'd have a great excuse for bright red skin. In the meantime, she didn't have to talk to Spence at all.

He didn't seem to notice the omission. The only sounds in the room were the soft whisper of Sharley's brush passing through the long golden strands of hair, the crackle of the flames consuming another oak log and an occasional snap as a piece of the puzzle went into place.

After a few minutes, Spence got up and went back to his bedroom.

I won, Sharley thought. I outlasted him. But there was little sense of victory.

Her hair was almost dry. She sat there for a short while longer, running the brush slowly through each lock till the whole mass of hair lay gleaming and golden against her pale blue sweater. Then she put the brush down and stared into the fire, trying to calculate how long this was likely to go on.

Though the wind had died, she didn't have to look far for evidence that the temperature had not risen much; the windows were still ice-coated. Back in Hammond's Point, she knew, the road crews would have been spreading sand and salt as soon as the storm started, and by now the streets would be almost back to normal. But out here, there were too many roads and too few residents to make that sort of program cost-effective. With the closest neighbor a mile away, and the cabin closed up entirely during most winters, it would be a wonder if they saw a maintenance truck before May. Of course, the ice would come off naturally long before that. The first time the sun began to shine, it would start to melt....

She didn't hear Spence come back, and she didn't even know he was in the main room until a blast of cold air swirled through the front door and wrapped itself around her. "Hey," she said, craning her neck in an effort to see what he was looking at, "you're letting all the heat out."

"I'm trying to see what shape the road's in." He shut the door with a bang.

Sharley told herself she shouldn't be surprised to find him just as eager for escape as she was. "Don't get your hopes up. I heard Joe Baxter say once that they use the religious system of snow removal up here."

Spence's eyebrows rose quizzically. "What's that?"

"As he defined it, 'The good Lord put it there, and the good Lord will take it away in His own time.' I suspect it's even more true when it comes to ice."

Spence shrugged. "Let's go out and see what it's like."

"Feel free." Sharley picked up her brush again.

He came to stand over her, feet spread, arms crossed. "It might be a good idea to use the buddy system."

"Why? So we can fall down together?"

"The fresh air and exercise would do us both good."

She looked up at that. "What about your cold?"

Spence shrugged. "I'm fine today. It must not have been a full-fledged cold, just exposure to the wind and damp."

"So as soon as you're feeling better, you want to go get another dose of it," Sharley grumbled.

"What are you, anyway? Lazy?" He bent over and seized her wrists, and before Sharley realized what he was doing she was on her feet. "A little walk will do you a world of good. You'll appreciate your food, too." He guided her toward the back door and wrapped a scarf around her face.

"I already do." Sharley's voice was muffled; she pushed the scarf down.

"That's true," Spence said thoughtfully. "You're one of the few women I know who isn't always sighing about how many calories something contains."

"Thank Charlotte for that." She submitted to having her coat put on. "She told me once that since the entire subject of weight watching is excruciatingly boring for everyone except the dieter, a lady doesn't discuss it."

"Hurray for Charlotte." He zipped his own parka and pulled the door open.

Sharley shivered and pulled a pair of furry earmuffs from her pocket. The wind might have died, but there was still a blast of cold, and after the cozy warmth of the cabin, it felt downright unpleasant.

Her feet were unsteady on the icy porch, and she braced herself with one hand on the woodpile. With the number of trips Spence had made out here for firewood, she thought, it was a wonder he hadn't fallen. She could scarcely walk even though she could see exactly where she was going. How had he managed in the dark with his arms full of logs?

Sharley picked her way down the steps and stopped to look around.

Heavy clouds still hung low in the sky, and without the brilliance of sunshine, all the color seemed to have been drained out of the landscape. It looked like a stark monochrome photograph, with everything in black and white and infinite shades of gray. And it was just as still; she could see no sign of animal life or birds or humans.

"Great place to park a car, Collins," Spence called, and she turned a little too fast and had to fight for her balance. She slid a couple of feet and smacked into the passenger door.

Spence was leaning against the front fender, arms crossed. "Didn't it occur to you that it might be wiser to leave the car on a solid surface," he asked politely, "instead of driving it down a hill and onto a patch of grass?"

"That's humorous, coming from someone who left his car in a ditch."

"I didn't do that on purpose. And I want you to know I made it considerably farther than the average driver."

"The average driver would probably have been smart enough to turn around," Sharley muttered.

"There was no place wide enough," Spence said calmly, "or I would have."

And then she would have been alone out here. Of course, there was no sense in pursuing that line of thought.

She studied the angle at which the car sat. Spence was right about the hill; why hadn't she considered that fact the night she'd arrived? "It doesn't have ice underneath," she pointed out. "I can get a run ..."

"What good do you think that'll do? Unless you can get up enough momentum within twenty feet to get over that hump, I believe your car is here to stay for a while."

Sharley thought about trying to push it out and con-cluded it was a lost cause. She shrugged. "All I could think of that night was getting my supplies inside without drowning." Her voice was apologetic. "It never occurred to me it was going to freeze."

Spence sighed. "Well, it's done now. Let's go see how bad mine is."

Sharley didn't have the heart to protest. After all, she was hardly in any position to criticize his crazy ideas; if she'd been a bit more sensible, at least they would have had a hope of getting out soon. Besides, she told herself, per-haps Spence's car wasn't in as bad a spot as he'd thought. Everything looked worse in the dark, didn't it? Maybe they could get it out of the ditch and go back to town right now.

Once they reached the gravel road, the going was a little easier; the rocks were ice-coated and treacherous, but at least it wasn't like walking on a sheet of polished steel. The gentle hills, however, seemed to be magnified by the coat-ing of ice. Sharley was breathing hard by the time they reached the top of the first slope, and the frigid air made her lungs ache. "How much farther?" she asked.

Spence shook his head. "I'm not sure. I started count-ing hills, but it got too depressing so I gave it up."

"How many did you count before you quit?"

"Four."

"Thanks a lot," Sharley said under her breath.

Spence grinned. "You asked."

The farther they went, the more debris they saw scat-tered across the road. Sharley had heard a few branches give way outside the cabin, but for the first time she be-gan to realize the extent of the damage the storm had done. The broken branches ranged in size from twigs to sapling-size boughs to limbs as big around as her waist, wrenched from the trees by the sheer dead weight of the ice. Now and then, the crackle of their footsteps was echoed by the snap of yet another branch giving way.

Sharley crossed the road to take a closer look at one big limb, and Spence's hand shot out and pulled her back. "Watch out for electrical wires," he warned. "They could be tangled up anywhere."

"But the power's out."

"Yes, but that doesn't mean something couldn't still be hot. I doubt it, but just in case . . ."

Sharley kept her distance from the fallen branches after that, watching each step and trying not to think about the warmth of Spence's hand still holding her arm, and how much she wished he was holding her hand, instead.

As walks went, it wasn't an unpleasant one. The air was cold, but she was getting used to it. She was well wrapped up, and there was no wind to cut through her coat and jeans. And Spence had been right about the benefit of some exercise; she'd had a bit of a nagging headache earlier, so little that she'd hardly realized it. It had come from sitting too close to the fire, she supposed, a combination of heat and eyestrain from looking directly at the flames as she dried her hair. But it was gone now.

She had lost track of distance by the time Spence stopped at the brink of a hill and groaned.

Halfway up the next hill was his car, nose-down in the ditch. Even from this distance Sharley could see that both front fenders were crumpled, and one of the back wheels wasn't even touching the ground.

So much for the idea of just backing it onto the road. That mess was going to take a tow truck and then a small fortune at a body shop.

Not that it couldn't have been a whole lot worse, she realized. Another couple of feet, and the car would have broken through a line of brush and gone down into a ravine. Spence would have been lucky to get out at all, much less in good enough shape to walk a mile to the cabin. He could have died right there, in a mass of twisted metal, or of the cold, if he hadn't been able to seek shelter.

She could feel the blood draining from her face as the shock sank in. He had been in terrible danger.

"Well, that's about the way I remembered it," Spence said. "Pretty impressive, wouldn't you say?"

Sharley swallowed hard. The danger was past, she reminded herself. And besides, what happened to him wasn't her business anymore. "Great place to park a car, Greenfield," she deadpanned. "I'm glad I have an excuse not to lend you mine."

Spence gave her a crooked grin and turned back toward the cabin.

"Aren't you going over to check on it at least?" she asked.

He shrugged. "Who's going to steal it? Besides, even if we could get it out, didn't you see the tree at the top of—"

He stopped, and in the split second of silence that followed, Sharley heard a crack like that of a high-powered rifle. She started to look around for its source.

That was why she never saw what hit her. She felt an abrupt sensation of flying, as if she was suddenly weightless, and the next thing she knew she was lying flat on the gravel, several feet from where she had been standing, with Spence crouched protectively over her.

She turned her head awkwardly and saw branches, instead of the gravel she had expected, within inches of her face. The branches seemed to be swaying, but she wasn't certain if they were actually moving or if her head was swimming from the impact of hitting the icy gravel.

She tried to speak, but the breath had been knocked from her lungs and all she could do was wheeze.

"Sharley," Spence said anxiously, and shook her. "Are you all right?"

His touch was gentle, but Sharley felt as if her teeth were rattling. It took another minute before she could speak. "I'm fine," she managed to say. "I've just... never been tackled before."

"I didn't have much choice, you know. You crazy fool, standing there watching the damned thing come straight at you...." He pushed himself up till he was kneeling beside her. "Lie still for a minute and let me check you over. I didn't expect you to go down so hard. Guess I forgot about the ice underfoot."

His hands felt warm, even through her thick coat. Sharley asked, more to distract herself than because she wanted to know, "Was that the tree you were talking about?"

He shook his head impatiently. "No. I meant the one at the top of the next hill over there, which has already done the same thing this one just did."

"You mean, fall?" she said uncertainly.

"You finally noticed." But the mocking note in his voice was a little shaky. "Sharley—"

"Oh, Spence." She reached for him with an almost convulsive strength, locking her arms around his neck and pulling him down to her as if he were a blanket that could warm and comfort and heal her.

His cheek brushed hers. The stubble of his beard felt softer than she'd expected, not much scratchier than the flutter of his eyelashes against her temple.

She started to shudder uncontrollably with the realization of how close that branch had come to knocking her out—or knocking her dead.

Spence's mouth brushed her cheek. "It's all right," he whispered. "It's all right."

She didn't let go. Her fingers laced together at the back of his neck, and she turned her face into the warm curve of his neck.

"Dammit," he said unsteadily. "I thought if I got you outside I wouldn't be so tempted to do this."

Sharley didn't ask; she didn't need to. And there wasn't time to wonder if this was right, or wise. She arched her back a little and tugged, and Spence let her hands against the nape of his neck pull him down to her.

His mouth was cold, but within moments the chill had gone, banished by a hungry heat that seemed to weld them together till nothing else had any reality.

Abruptly Spence pulled away. He was breathing hard, and his eyes were cloudy. "There's no sense in playing with fire," he muttered.

Sharley sagged against the gravel.

After a moment, Spence soberly helped her to her feet. "Ready to go back?"

She nodded and swallowed hard. "I'm sorry, Spence." He didn't answer, and she thought for a moment he hadn't heard.

"Not your fault," he said finally. "It's a good thing you weren't wearing shorts. You'd have been a mass of gravel burns."

For some insane reason, the image of herself wearing shorts in weather like this and being struck by a tree weighed down by ice struck Sharley as comical, and she hugged herself and bent over and howled with laughter.

"Sharley, cut it out." His voice was firm.

She could hardly talk. "But that's hysterically funny! With sandals and sunglasses, no doubt, and a beach towel over my shoulder..."

"The operative word is 'hysterical,' I agree with that much. Come on. I think the cold and the shock . . . and everything have affected your brain."

Sharley sobered abruptly, and her eyes filled with tears.

Spence retrieved her earmuffs from under a small branch at the side of the road. "I'm sorry I hurt you."

She shook her head vehemently. "Don't be an idiot, Spence. You saved my life. At least kept me from getting a really nasty bump on the head."

His hand brushed the nape of her neck and then slid up into her hair, his fingers spread to gently probe as much of the back of her skull as he could. Sharley held her breath.

"I'm not so sure about the bump," he said. "You don't look concussed, but you're acting that way."

Sharley thought he might be right; the touch of his fingertips, gentle though it was, was like sandpaper on her scalp. She didn't know whether to be relieved or disappointed when his hand dropped back to his side.

"What made the tree fall, anyway?" she asked. "Right then, I mean. Or was it just my bad luck in choosing the wrong spot to stand?"

"It might have been like an avalanche, I suppose," Spence mused. "The tree was weakened by the tremendous weight of all that ice, and sooner or later something had to give. But perhaps we caused a vibration that brought it all down right then."

Sharley frowned. "Just by walking past, you mean?"

"Or talking."

"Like singing a high note and breaking glass?"

"Something like that. It's an interesting physics question."

She managed a giggle. "All those voice lessons Charlotte insisted I take finally had some effect!"

The walk back seemed infinitely longer, and when they reached the cabin Sharley heaved a gigantic sigh of relief. "I'm as sleepy as a baby after all that fresh air," she announced. "I think I'll—"

"Sorry, but no naps."

"Why not?" She studied him closely while she unbuttoned her coat and hung it up. "Oh, I know. But you don't really think I have a concussion, do you?"

"I hope not, but there's no sense in taking a chance."

"I don't know what you'd do about it if I passed out, anyway," she complained. "You couldn't carry me all the way to the Baxters' place."

"I could drag you by the hair," Spence said. "How about some coffee to help keep you awake?"

Sharley shrugged and sat down by the fire, wincing a little as the most sensitive parts of her body protested. Until that moment, she had thought every muscle had been equally abused in her fall. "How do football players stand up to this? I can't imagine volunteering for this kind of treatment." She curled up in an almost fetal position and closed her eyes.

"Enough of that," Spence called. "There's a deck of cards in that cabinet if you'd like to play poker."

Sharley sighed. "Do I have a choice?" She stayed exactly where she was until he set two cups of coffee down near her and nudged her gently on the shoulder.

"Wake up, sleeping beauty," he said. "Or shall I grab a handful of hair and start dragging?"

Sharley sat up. "Does it have to be poker?"

"I could be persuaded to make it something else, instead."

"Crazy eights," Sharley decided.

"Why that, for heaven's sake?"

She gave him a gamin smile. "Because I've had so much practice with seven-year-olds on cold and snowy days that I can play it in my sleep."

Spence laughed and pulled up a chair. "Unfortunately for you, I am not a seven-year-old." He retrieved the cards and shuffled them expertly. "What keeps you enthusiastic in the classroom, anyway? After three years of teaching the same math lessons and the same reading, I'd think it would get dull."

"Looking at it that way does make it sound boring," Sharley admitted. "But as a matter of fact, I don't teach lessons at all." She gathered up her cards and began sorting them.

Spence looked stunned. "What does that mean? How can you not teach—"

"I teach *kids*. And even if the subject matter is the same, no two days are ever alike, because the kids are different."

Spence set the remainder of the pack down between them. He did not rush to pick up his cards. "You never told me that before. I had no idea you felt that way about your job."

Sharley didn't look up from her cards. "You never asked," she said, and put a king down on the discard pile.

How little we really knew about each other, she thought, when we committed our lives to each other forever! Perhaps it was just as well, after all, that things had turned out as they had.

But no matter how true it might be, that fact didn't wash the sadness out of her heart.

CHAPTER SIX

SHARLEY REARRANGED her cards with unnecessary care, until she could trust herself to smile brightly as she looked up. "Aren't you going to play?"

Spence hadn't even picked up his cards. He was leaning back in his chair, one long-fingered hand idly rubbing the dark stubble of beard as if it itched, studying her. "You're right," he said quietly. "There never seemed to be time. If you weren't busy with school or with wedding plans, you were filling in for Charlotte in all her social commitments."

"Oh?" Sharley said crisply. "And you never had anything on your own calendar, I suppose?"

Spence smiled a little. "Guilty. So I'm asking now. What makes you a teacher? And why such little kids?"

"Oh, you sound like Charlotte. What does it matter, anyway?" Then she thought better of it. Who knew how long they would be stuck with each other's company? At least talking helped fill the hours. "I've always wanted to teach," she said slowly. "Before I could even read, I used to line up my teddy bears and give them lessons."

There was a mischievous quirk at the corner of his mouth. "What did you do when they got out of line? Make them sit in a corner for a week?"

Sharley pretended not to hear. "And I always wanted to teach little kids. Second grade is just about perfect, I think. The kids have learned to get along with one another."

Spence played a card. "As much as they're ever going to, I suppose."

"What a cynical attitude. They've learned the essentials—I'm not sure I'd be so good at teaching shoe-tying." But the fact was, she reminded herself, she'd looked forward to someday teaching one child—her child—to tie his shoes, and recognize his colors and count to ten. One very special child, or maybe two. But there was no point in dreaming now of what might have been if only things had turned out differently.

She took a deep breath and plunged on. "By the time they're seven, their attention span has developed and they're ready to look out at the world. A second grader is really just a big bump of curiosity with an appetite attached, you know."

Spence laughed.

"It's true," Sharley protested. She wasn't quite sure whether to be happy that he hadn't noticed her hesitation, or annoyed because he obviously hadn't even thought of the children they might have had together. *Be happy,* she commanded herself. It was much less painful that way.

"And that's what you find so fascinating?"

She nodded. "There's a magic about opening a child's window to life. It's a thrill like nothing else on earth."

"You almost make me want to try it myself," he mused. "What did you mean about Charlotte?"

"Nothing, really. She's just never understood my choice of careers."

Spence nodded. "Silly job, teaching." He almost caught the inflection of Charlotte's voice.

Sharley smiled despite herself at the imitation. "Well, her objection isn't quite that strong. At least teaching is a ladylike occupation—better than a lot of other things I could have chosen."

"Steelworker," Spence murmured. "Forensic pathologist. Barroom singer. Yes, she has a point."

"But if I insist on teaching, she says, why must I waste my life with children? Why not nice college-aged boys and girls, and a professorship that has some status and a future?"

"Well," Spence said reasonably, "why not?"

Sharley shot him a look.

"Don't glare at me as if I've just scuttled your lifeboat," he ordered. "I'm only asking. Are you certain you want to play that card?"

Sharley glanced at it. "Too late now."

"I'll let you take it back, but you owe me one."

She shook her head. "I think I'll let it stand. Why not college? Because anybody can teach those people."

"I beg your pardon, but—"

"Think about it, Spence. By the time someone gets to college age, he either wants to learn or he doesn't. If he does, he can practically teach himself. If he doesn't, he's going to skip class and party—and what sort of teachers he has won't matter much."

He shook his head. "I'm not sure I agree with that. I remember a few teachers—"

He stopped, and after a moment Sharley prompted, "Yes?"

Spence said slowly, "My last year of high school, there was a teacher who gave me a really rough time. I was pretty much the kind of kid you were describing—the sort who always had an excuse, instead of his homework, and who sometimes didn't even bother with the excuse."

Sharley nodded.

"My mother had died that year and there just didn't seem to be anything important about school. I certainly didn't expect it to lead to anything, and in fact I was thinking about quitting."

"But—"

"I planned to end up working on cars. It seemed to be the only thing I had a talent for, so why shouldn't I get started?"

"A bit shortsighted," Sharley murmured.

"Maybe, but I was eighteen and it didn't look as if there were any alternatives. I didn't have an adoring aunt and uncle volunteering to pay for my college education."

Sharley bit her lip. He hadn't sounded sarcastic, exactly, and surely he must realize that she knew how very lucky she was. Still . . .

"At any rate, I thought this teacher just had it in for me till she called me in one afternoon and laid the facts on the line. She told me that what happened to my father wasn't enough of an excuse for me to waste my life."

Sharley drew a long, shocked breath.

Spence grinned crookedly. "I told her if she'd been a man I'd have hit her, and she said she'd suspected I must have a sense of honor hidden somewhere and I'd just showed her where it was."

"She was a pretty cool customer."

"Very. She knew every pressure point and exactly how hard to push to get the desired result. After I'd studied a little psychology in college I could see exactly what she'd been up to, but that day, well, all I knew was that it was the first time anybody seemed to care. It was the first time someone held out a dream and said, 'This can be yours, Spence.'"

Sharley put her hand over his.

Spence didn't look at her. "That's the first time I've told anybody about her."

She could tell by his voice that he regretted it, too—at least partly—for fear that she would drown him in maudlin sympathy. She had to clear her throat before she could say, "But that proves my point, Spence. If you'd already been in college, that teacher might never have had a chance to know you well enough to figure out which buttons to push."

He smiled a little at that.

"So you were going to work on cars," Sharley mused. "Engines or bodies?"

"Engines. Why?"

"Too bad. The way your car looks, it's going to need a good body man." Sharley studied her remaining cards. "Or maybe two of them," she added thoughtfully.

"No doubt I messed up the engine, as well. It hit pretty hard."

"Oh, that makes me feel much better." Her voice was faintly ironic.

Spence smiled again and played his final card. "Thanks, Sharley."

"For what? The concern or the opportunity to trounce me? By the way, are you talking to me to check whether I'm still making sense or to distract me from playing well?"

"Both." Spence gathered up the cards and started to shuffle. "And it seems to be working. Are you sure you don't want to play poker?"

"I'm sure." She pulled herself up from the depths of the couch. It wasn't easy; the cushions sagged, and her body ached all over. Perhaps sitting still hadn't been such a wonderful idea; moving around might have kept her muscles loose. "I want something to eat. We never had breakfast."

"Speak for yourself."

She paused on her way to the kitchen and looked over her shoulder at him. "Is that why you were rummaging around the cabin this morning and making so much noise?"

"Rummaging?" He sounded offended. "I'll have you know I was very quiet."

Sharley cut a thick slice from a loaf of bread and spread jam on it. "Why? So I wouldn't demand that you share?"

"I resent that accusation. Of course I'd have shared." He'd come over and was leaning against the kitchen counter by then, watching as she nibbled at her slice of bread. "Are you going to?"

"Share? Fix it yourself, Spence. But I'll make you a cup of coffee." She refilled the kettle and put it on the stove.

"Only because you want one."

"That's the true spirit of cooperation, wouldn't you say?"

Spence reached for the bread knife. "If that's the case, I shouldn't tell you that you have jam on your face."

Sharley wiped at the corner of her mouth.

Spence shook his head. "You missed."

"Where exactly?"

He was leisurely spreading jam on his bread, making sure every molecule of the surface was covered. "Come here and I'll show you. Out of the goodness of my heart, you understand."

He wasn't looking at her, but the slightly gruff note in his voice made Sharley's insides flutter just a little. He couldn't mean he intended to kiss the silly smear off her face—could he? After what he had said about playing with fire? No, of course he didn't intend any such thing.

She didn't realize she had moved toward him until he turned to face her. The kitchen was chilly, but Spence's breath was warm against her forehead. Warm, and a little faster than normal—almost as it had been out there on the hilltop.

His arm was half encircling her. Sharley's stomach did a somersault. You know better, she told herself. But she closed her eyes, anyway, and waited for the touch of his mouth against hers.

But instead, she felt the chilly brush of fabric against her chin, and her eyelids flew open just as Spence drew a damp kitchen towel back from her face. "There," he said matter-of-factly. "That takes care of it." He tossed the towel over Sharley's shoulder toward the sink and went back to spreading his jam with infinite care.

That, she told herself, will teach you to think you're irresistible.

She ate the rest of her bread slowly, taking small bites because the loaf was beginning to get dry and it threatened to choke her. Then she made the coffee.

But she was still thinking about the jam. She was overreacting to the whole situation, of course, she told herself. Spence was right about the dangers of playing with fire. This whole mess was bad enough as it was. To add physical contact was like turning up the flame of a Bunsen burner under a beaker of acid. Only an idiot did that.

That knowledge didn't stop her from being an idiot, she reflected. It was almost as if that stunning kiss out on the hilltop had taken the lid off a box inside her mind—a little hiding place where she had hidden away the memories of every kiss, every caress, every touch. Now those memories were pouring out again, and everything he did seemed to strike a chord and call up an image. . . .

Physical attraction isn't everything, she told herself firmly. It wasn't even the most important thing in a relationship. So why was she allowing herself to drown in old desires?

Habit, that was all. She simply must get her thinking straightened out before it caused even more trouble.

Spence was searching through the food in the cabinet, and his off-key whistle was about to drive her around the bend by the time he decided on a can of ready-to-eat soup.

"Let's have an early lunch," he suggested. "Just to make up for the late breakfast. Where's the can opener?"

Sharley tugged at the drawer where she'd stashed it. When the drawer stuck, she pulled harder, and the porcelain knob came off in her hand. She stood there for a moment looking incredulously from the handle to the drawer. The kitchen was old, and the drawer fronts were built flush with the face of the cabinets; there wasn't even an edge to get hold of.

It was bad enough to be without refrigeration, she thought, but if they couldn't get to the can opener, things were quickly going from bad to worse.

Spence turned around impatiently with one hand extended for the can opener, and his eyes narrowed. "Now what?"

Sharley shrugged and held up the knob. "Hand me the bread knife and I'll try to pry it open."

"And probably slit your wrists doing it." He pushed up his sweater sleeves and pulled open the next drawer down, sliding both hands inside it and pressing his palms against the bottom of the troublemaker. "Wooden runners," he said. "That figures. They've warped or swelled somehow."

The drawer groaned stubbornly, and Sharley watched as the tendons in his forearms tensed and strained. Finally the drawer creaked open an inch. Spence slid his fingers into the gap and yanked, but could only get it open another inch.

"Damn," he said. "Can you get your hand in there? Mine's too big."

Sharley slipped both hands in and managed to snag the can opener. She had to dangle the tool between her index fingers and turn it at an angle to fit it through the narrow opening.

"No problem," Spence said cheerfully. "If there's anything else in there we might need, you may as well dig it out now. I doubt that drawer will open again till June."

Sharley fumbled around. "I'll have to remember this little exercise for my kids at school. It's a challenge to identify shapes without seeing them— Ouch!"

"Watch out for knives," Spence warned.

"Now you tell me. I wouldn't have thought we'd have sticky drawers in the winter, would you? It should be dry as tinder in here with the stove running and the fire blazing."

"It's probably all the water we've been boiling."

Sharley shrugged. "One must have coffee."

"Still, it's a wonder anything works at all in this cabin, you know. It's cold all winter, probably full of mildew in summer and neglected all year around. A little work with a plane, and that drawer would never be any trouble again, but Martin would never think of doing that."

Sharley gave up on the contents of the drawer and studied the knuckle she'd skinned. "Well, no one ever accused Martin of being mechanically inclined. The last time he tried to mow the lawn he mixed the oil with the gas to save time and ruined the mower."

"When was that?"

"Oh, five years or so ago. That was when Charlotte hired the handyman."

"Figures." Spence tossed the loose knob into the drawer.

Sharley started to protest, then thought better of it. He'd probably tell her that if she wanted it back, she could dig it out. "Is that why Martin is so fond of you?" she asked. "Because you do things like that so skillfully?"

"Getting that drawer open wasn't skill, Sharley, it was brute strength. And I'd hate to think that's the only reason Martin keeps me around." The comment sounded almost absentminded.

Sharley perched on the corner of the table. "You know," she said cautiously, "I've always wondered why you stayed in Hammond's Point."

He glanced at her and then turned back to stirring the soup. "Hudson Products was a good opportunity for me, sort of a mix between people management and practical problem-solving. I'm a hands-on kind of guy myself, but in most companies that size I'd never get onto the production floor."

Sharley let the silence drag out for half a minute, but he didn't seem inclined to continue. "No, I meant—" She stopped. "Sorry. It's none of my business."

"Because of my father, you mean, and what he did?"

It was the first time Sharley could ever remember that he'd opened the subject. "Well . . . yes. I'd have thought it would be easier somewhere else."

Spence shrugged. "I almost went away. I was practically blacklisted in Hammond's Point, that's for sure. Nobody was willing to take much of a risk on John Greenfield's kid. But I couldn't quite forget something that teacher told me—that I couldn't run away from what had happened, because no matter where I went I had to live with myself. So when Martin gave me a chance . . ." His voice cracked a little.

"He's a pretty special guy, isn't he?" Sharley said softly. "I certainly can't ever forget how much I owe him. Charlotte, too, of course, but Martin isn't family, at least not the way Charlotte is. She's my mother's sister. He didn't have to take me in and treat me like his own, but he did.''

"Yeah," Spence said flatly. "I know."

She wondered exactly what he meant by that, but before she could even begin to speculate, Spence continued, "You're even named for Charlotte, aren't you?"

"Sort of. I had a godmother named Shirley, so it was an effort to include them both. Look!"

Spence jumped and swore as hot soup splashed onto his hand. "What?"

"The sun's shining." Sharley rushed to the window. It had escaped the worst of the ice, and so the center of the glass was still clear, obscured only by condensation on the inside. She grabbed the kitchen towel to wipe the moisture off, and grimaced at the resulting dirty stain on the towel. How long had it been since the windows had been washed, anyway?

The light was pale and weak, but it was undeniably direct sun. It looked to Sharley as if color had suddenly come back into a black-and-white world, and shadows added depth and dimension to what had seemed an eerily flat and simplistic landscape. The ice coating on the branches gleamed like elongated diamonds and scattered tiny rainbows across the hillside.

Spence had followed her to the window. "It won't be long now before it starts to melt, will it?" Sharley said. In her enthusiasm, she grabbed his arm and gave it a shake. "Maybe we can even get out today!"

"If this keeps up." He craned his neck toward the west. "I can't tell if the sky is clearing or if that's just a momentary break in the clouds."

But even as he spoke, the shadows faded and blinked into oblivion, as if they had never been.

Sharley wailed, "Dammit, it isn't fair!"

"It's only been a day. It's not forever." Spence's voice was dry.

She realized abruptly that she had let her head drop against his shoulder, and she jerked away. "Sorry."

"What are shoulders for?" he said. "The soup's hot. Are there some more crackers?"

She dug through the cabinets, grateful for the chance to keep her back turned. What was the matter with her, anyway? She didn't want the man; couldn't she even keep her hands off him?

Spence dished up the soup and said, "What shall we do after lunch? Do you want your revenge at crazy eights?"

Sharley seized at the change of subject. "More cards? No, thanks. I was getting blisters on my fingers from shuffling." And on my heart, she thought, from being too close to you. "I think I'll clean the place up a little."

Spence looked around. "Why bother?"

"Well, I don't expect I'll wipe out every speck of dirt. But ever since you mentioned the condition it's in..." She shuddered. "It's funny I hadn't really noticed before."

"No, it's not. The light's so dim in here you wouldn't see a snake unless you tripped over it."

"Oh, that's reassuring! I suppose when I used to come up here with Martin I didn't notice whether the place was clean because I was just a kid. Or maybe he had Mrs. Baxter give the place a good scrubbing now and then. Somehow I don't think Joe is the kind who sees cobwebs till they're big enough to strangle him."

Spence grinned. "I think I'll go looking for the main woodpile. I don't know if you've noticed, but we've made an awful dent in the one by the back door, and if the temperature drops again tonight we'll need extra."

At least scrubbing the kitchen gave her something to do. It occupied her mind more fully than simply sitting by the fire would have, and she attacked the dirt with fierce energy. But activity did not eliminate the headache that had been nagging at her all day. Now and then, she had to stop to rest and catch her breath, and almost every time she glanced out the window she saw Spence stacking yet another armful of wood on the back porch. He didn't seem to be in any hurry to get back inside. Despite the temperature, he even stopped now and then to study the sky—or perhaps he was watching the birds. Had he been as anxious to escape her as she had to keep her distance from him?

He carried the last load of logs inside, along with a metal bucket, and carefully scooped the built-up ashes out of the fireplace before starting a fresh fire.

Sharley finally gave up on the dirt and sank onto the couch, closing her eyes. Her head was aching in earnest now, and she felt a little sick to her stomach, too.

Finally Spence pushed himself back from the fireplace, where a new little blaze crackled cheerfully. "Sorry about the mess I'm making."

Sharley didn't open her eyes. "It doesn't bother me if you scatter ashes all over the room. I only got the kitchen done."

"You look exhausted."

"Oh, my neck is a little sore, and I've got a bit of a headache."

He frowned. "From the fall?"

She shook her head, carefully. "No. I had the headache when I woke up this morning. I took some aspirin earlier, but it doesn't seem to be doing any good."

"Let me put these ashes outside and wash my hands, and I'll give you a neck rub."

By the time he came back to the living room, Sharley was almost asleep, stretched out on her stomach on the couch. He sat down on the edge of the cushion beside her, and she murmured a halfhearted protest at being disturbed. Spence ignored the complaint and began to rub her neck.

His hands were warm and firm and strong, and soon the gentle pressure brought an answering heat from deep inside her muscles. It was soothing and relaxing, and she made a little whimpering noise deep in her throat.

Spence's fingers stilled. "Did I hurt you?"

"No." She had to make an effort to speak at all. "At least, it was a good sort of pain. Besides," she added childishly, "it's the least you can do. After all, you're the reason I feel lousy."

"Me? Oh, the way I tackled you."

Sharley shook her head and then wished she hadn't; the headache had not gone away. "I think it's more than that. I'm not just achy all over, I feel almost sick, too. You must have given me your cold."

"It wasn't a cold. Haven't you noticed I'm not even sneezing anymore?"

"Well, yesterday you looked the way I feel right now," Sharley said stubbornly. "Maybe it's the flu and you only had a touch of it."

But it was too much effort to argue about it, so she closed her eyes again and let herself sink into the cushions, driven by the gently relentless pressure of his fingers. She had never realized before that his hands were so strong. But then, there had never been a time when he had touched her with anything but tenderness. Even now, he wasn't being rough or harsh; his fingers searched out every sore muscle in her neck and shoulders and squeezed the pain away, but it wasn't a hurtful touch. Instead, it was almost sensual.

As if he'd read her mind, Spence gave a final quick brush to the nape of her neck. "That's all my fingers can take," he said.

Had there been an odd catch in his voice? Sharley turned over slowly so she could look up at him.

He was rubbing his eyes as if they hurt. "I must have gotten soot in them," he muttered.

"And rubbing them is really going to help." Sharley caught at his arm. "Cut it out, Spence, before you blind yourself."

He gave her a rueful grin.

"On the other hand," she said softly, "you might not look at all bad with an eye patch. Between that and the beard, you could be a pirate." Almost unconsciously, she raised a hand to rub the stubble of his beard.

"Sharley," he said softly.

But Sharley didn't hear the warning in his voice. A rebellious little imp in the back of her brain had taken over. This should have been your honeymoon, it whispered. The phrase was almost like a mantra, echoing through her head.

Her fingertip brushed the cleft in his chin, and her palm curved around his cheek. He caught her hand and pulled it away, but his fingers interlocked with hers, and as he gently pushed her hand back to her side, he bent almost automatically toward her. His lips were parted a little.

Sharley's eyes closed slowly.

He released her fingers, but only to slip both his hands under her shoulders to raise her into a half-sitting position. She braced her hands against his shoulders, relishing his strength.

"You are so very beautiful." His voice was barely more than a whisper, warm against her lips, and his kiss was soft and seeking, the kind of caress that so often during their engagement had made her want to forget that inconvenient promise to herself to wait until her wedding day.

Sharley's fingers crept past his jaw, over his ear, through his hair. What would be so terrible about giving in to that desire? *This should have been your honeymoon....*

But it wasn't, and for very good reason.

She pulled back a little, and instantly Spence let her go. He twisted around on the edge of the couch till his back was to her and started to rub his temples, as if his head hurt, too. "Dammit, Sharley, would you cut out the games?"

She bit her lip. She couldn't honestly deny the accusation that she'd started it—and yet it hadn't been all her doing. "And I suppose that neck rub wasn't premeditated?" she snapped.

Spence didn't answer. He moved away from the couch, though, and she could tell from the tiny noises that he had knelt to add a log to the fire.

"How long do you think it will be till we get out?" she asked.

"Tomorrow, I'd say. We'll chance it, anyway."

Because we can't stay here together any longer. She could almost hear him saying it, it rang so clearly through her head. Or had she said it herself?

Sharley pushed herself up to sit on the edge of the couch. Suddenly it seemed very important that Spence not think she was incapable of controlling herself. "I'm anxious about Charlotte, you know," she said almost at random. "I didn't tell her I wasn't going to the resort. I didn't even stop to think of how much she'll fret if she tries to call there and I haven't turned up. I must have been crazy not to think of her before now."

Spence didn't turn around. "No wonder if you were. Crazy, I mean."

"What does that mean?"

"The urge to get away from Charlotte must be almost a primal drive."

"Why? I love Charlotte. She's been very good to me."

"She's really got you buffaloed, doesn't she? I'm amazed that, instead of just whining about your teaching career, she didn't try to keep you from doing anything at all."

"Why would she have done that?" Sharley stood up and paced across the main room. "I have to do something to make a living."

"Oh, really?" His tone was dry.

Sharley's voice tightened. "Even if Martin and Charlotte plan to leave me every cent they have, which I'm not at all sure they intend to do, I'd still want some kind of career. I've always been determined to do something important with my life."

Spence nodded. "Of course. That's why she's had to take the long way around."

"What do you mean?"

"Hasn't it ever occurred to you that your precious aunt Charlotte would dearly love to have you sitting attentively by her side day and night?"

"Of course she wouldn't," Sharley said. "She's a sick woman, but she hates to take me away from my own plans."

"Oh? I never noticed her illness stopping her from doing anything she really wanted to do."

"That's absurd! She nearly died last fall."

"I'm not disputing that. But she'd be in better general health if she'd get up and do something, instead of lying on a couch swallowing pills and feeling sorry for herself."

"You have no idea how—"

"If she wants to shut herself off from the world, that's her business. But when she tries to manage your life, it's a different thing. Whose idea was it to renovate the gardener's cottage, anyway?"

"Charlotte's, of course," Sharley said stiffly.

"And before that, she suggested I just move into the house."

"That was absurd and she knew it! It was only a way of telling you how much she welcomed you." Tears stung Sharley's eyes, and she had to stop speaking because of the lump in her throat. It could have been so perfect, she thought.

"Was it?"

"Absurd? Of course it was. The house simply isn't big enough for two couples—"

"No. I meant, are you sure she was telling me how glad she was to have me in the family? Or was it a way to keep you as close to her as possible?"

"So now you're saying Charlotte opposed the whole idea? That's almost as ridiculous as saying she set up that scene so I'd walk in on you and break our engagement...." She looked at him levelly. "*Is* that what you're saying?"

Spence sighed. "No."

"Good. Because it would have been the stupidest suggestion ever." She turned her back on him. Her head was swimming from the strain. Perhaps she really was coming down with the flu; she certainly had all the symptoms.

"Sharley, please—"

"Are you asking me to forgive you, Spence?"

He didn't answer right away, and when he did, his voice was curt. "Not exactly."

"Because you didn't do anything, is that correct?" Her words dripped sarcasm. "You expect me to believe that, when I was there? I know what I saw, Spence!"

He dropped another log onto the fire with a crash that sent sparks and soot flying. "I don't expect anything from you anymore, Sharley."

"Good," she said.

Her headache was pounding even more fiercely now. That was no surprise. She would lie down for a while, till it abated, and then she would walk over to the Baxters' house. A mile wasn't so very far; she must have walked more than that this morning. At least then she would be away from the cabin. Away from Spence.

She sat down on the couch and let her head drop against the back cushions. "How could I have been so wrong about you?" she said, almost to herself.

Spence set the fire screen back in place. "I've been asking myself that question, too."

Silence fell, simple and painful, broken only by the occasional crackle of the fire.

CHAPTER SEVEN

SHARLEY WOULD SIMPLY HAVE gotten up and left the cabin right then if she'd had the energy. But she felt drained, as if she'd never have the strength to move again.

Why should this particular quarrel bother her so much, anyway? she asked herself. It was nothing compared to the first fight they'd had—the one that had ended their engagement. And in fact, this quarrel was only a continuation of that fight.

The first fight we ever had, she thought dreamily. In the two months of their engagement, they had never squabbled—not over wedding plans, not over the decoration of the cottage, not over what to do with the time they spent together....

She frowned a little. Had they never quarreled because they always agreed, or had their differences simply been covered up, buried? Spence's feelings about Charlotte certainly seemed to indicate a long-simmering resentment the existence of which Sharley had never even suspected. But there were other things, as well, now that she started to think about it, things less important in themselves, perhaps, than in the pattern they created. Had Spence really not cared what sort of china she chose, or had his apparent flexibility been part of a hidden agenda, a plan to keep Sharley happy at whatever cost? Had Charlotte been right to think that it wasn't Sharley herself that Spence had found so interesting, but Martin Hudson's niece?

Of course, if that was the game he'd been playing, everything had fallen apart that day in the gardener's cottage.

It didn't matter now, she reminded herself.

She thought about moving into her bedroom, where she could be as weak and weepy as she wanted. She hated being sick, and having to be around Spence made things even worse. If she could just crawl off in a corner and be wretched all by herself for a while... Damn the flu, anyway. Why did it have to hit her now?

Because your resistance is so low, she reminded herself. You're worn out and exhausted and upset.

Besides, the bug wouldn't be taking such a toll if she hadn't been emotionally wrung out to start with, and she had to admit that a few minutes ago—when Spence had kissed her—the headache and upset stomach and pain in her chest had almost disappeared.

Of course, nobody had ever said Spence wasn't good at that sort of thing, Sharley reflected. Since their first evening together at the Christmas party, he had always been able to knock every other thought out of her head, leaving room only for him. He could kiss her with a passion that left her smoldering and eager for the day she would be his bride—a passion that had made it terribly difficult for her not to lose her head.... Was that why he had turned to Wendy? For consolation and the expression of physical needs—because Sharley hadn't slept with him?

Don't twist yourself up in stupid questions. If that *was* why he had done it, she ought to be glad things had worked out as they had. Any man who honestly thought that was a good enough reason for having an affair was no fit candidate for a husband, that was certain.

And knowing all that, why did she still feel like crying?

She slept off and on for a couple of hours. But it didn't seem to matter; awake or dreaming, her mind ran in the same channels. Once, she heard herself say, "If you loved her, Spence, why did you ever propose to me?" and the shock of hearing the words echoing in her head sent her struggling upright on the couch.

But she'd only dreamed it. It must have been a dream, for when she looked around, Spence merely turned his head against the back of his chair and said, "What do you need, Sharley?"

"Nothing," she muttered, and lay down again, grateful that at least she hadn't blurted the question aloud. But her confusion didn't go away.

Had it been the money? The expectation that she would be Martin's heir, and so he would be assured not only of a job at Hudson Products but of eventual control of the company?

Her heart told her no; Spence wasn't the kind of man capable of that brand of cunning. And yet she could almost have understood if that had been the case. He'd had little security in his life until Martin had offered him a chance. Would it be any wonder if Spence had taken a hard look ahead and decided to solidify his position with the next owner of Hudson Products, too?

But he hadn't, Sharley told herself. The man she'd loved couldn't do that sort of thing. Spence really had cared about her; she could not bring herself to accept that she could have been so flagrantly deceived.

She shook her head restlessly and told herself not to be a fool; the man she'd loved had betrayed her. He'd never been the knight in shining armor she'd believed him to be.

The man she'd loved...and was he also the man she still loved, despite everything?

The sensation as she faced that question was like an earthquake shaking every cell of her body.

When a person truly loved, that emotion didn't simply disappear when the romance hit its first inevitable bump. And even when that first disillusionment was a massive one, as Sharley's had been, love didn't vanish in a twinkling. It might ebb and flow with the course of events, but it did not dry up and blow away like a garden herb in the first autumn breeze.

It'll take time to get over him, she'd told herself more than once in the past week. But what if no amount of time was enough? What if—despite the episode in the gardener's cottage, despite the breaking of her engagement, despite the harsh words and the quarrels—when it was all over, she found herself still loving him?

Loving him—and desperately wanting to trust him? Was it even possible that she could do what he had asked of her?

You'd take my word for it, if you loved me enough, he'd said.

But that brought her right back to the beginning. He expected her to believe he was innocent. Yet if he was, there must have been a reason for that episode in the cottage. So why on earth, if it could be explained, hadn't he told her what had really happened?

Sharley closed her eyes and deliberately let her mind slip back to that sunny afternoon when the world had still been bright and full of love and joy and promise. She had unlocked the door—or had she? She had used her key, she knew, but had the lock actually been fastened?

What difference does it make? she asked herself. If he'd expected to be discovered, he wouldn't have used the cottage at all. Obviously he had felt safe there, lock or no lock.

Sharley frowned. In the back of her mind a hazy impression had begun to form, and then vanished before she could grab at it.

She had walked into the tiny living room and noticed the new leather love seat, and the back of Spence's head, and Wendy's luxuriant hair cascading over his shoulder....

No, there hadn't been any mistake about that, either. Wendy had been in his arms, for when Spence had leapt to his feet, she had almost gone sliding onto the floor.

Perhaps Wendy had planned it that way, Sharley thought. Perhaps she had heard Sharley's approach and thrown herself into Spence's arms....

Sharley shook her head. You're grasping at straws, she told herself, trying to excuse him.

There simply hadn't been time for Wendy to manipulate the scene, and there had been nothing that suggested Spence could have been coerced into position, either. He'd been shocked when he first faced Sharley, all right, but obviously not by anything Wendy had done in the past few moments, for at the moment Sharley first saw him, before he even knew she was there, he had appeared quite comfortable. As a matter of fact, he looked as if he'd been sitting on the love seat for some time, with Wendy snuggled against him.

And what was it he had said? *It can't go on like this, Wendy*—something like that. No, obviously Spence had known exactly what he was dealing with. He wasn't even trying to reason with a cast-aside lover; it was plain as could be that he was laying down the law.

Yet somehow he hadn't sounded as if he was issuing an order. There had been a note of terrible pain in his voice, as if he was making an agonizing sacrifice.

But if it was Wendy he loved...

Sharley's head was pounding. *I have to stop this,* she told herself. *I have to get off this roller coaster.*

She let her head fall back against the cushions and admitted that she could string together all the logical excuses she liked, but it still wouldn't make any difference. If she argued it out inside herself for weeks, her head would still be telling her one thing and her heart another. And the truth was she wanted to believe her heart.

Because I still love him, she thought. *No matter what happened, or why he was there with her, I still love him.*

She groaned in pain, and Spence roused from his chair and came across to her to put his hand on her forehead. "You don't feel feverish," he said. "How about some orange juice? I think there's some left."

Sharley nodded. She pulled herself up till she was half sitting on the couch. The effort left her head swimming, and when Spence came back he rearranged the pillows at her back to prop her into place.

He had packed the glass with snow, and the cold liquid felt so soothing to her throat that Sharley swallowed half of it at a gulp. Then she realized that as long as she was drinking, Spence was likely to sit beside her, so she decided to sip the rest. Surely, if she dragged it out long enough, he would have to say something, wouldn't he?

Her own mind wasn't functioning clearly; she certainly had no witty repartee at her command, and no brilliant stroke of psychological insight into their problems, either. The lack annoyed her, and before she stopped to think she said brusquely, "I want to believe you. But how can I?"

She thought for a moment that he was going to ignore her completely. "I don't have any answer for that, Sharley. Either you can or you can't. Are you finished with the juice?"

"No, I'm not." She clutched the glass as if he was likely to snatch it. "Spence, please—just tell me what happened!"

His mouth tightened, but his voice was quiet. "It wouldn't do any good if I told you. And it would certainly make things worse."

Sharley gritted her teeth to hold back her tears. "I hate it when you act this way. You sound so damned reasonable, Spence Greenfield, when the truth is you might as well be speaking Martian for all the sense you make." Her hands were trembling so much that the orange juice threatened to slop over the edge of the glass.

He pried it out of her hand. "I know you think it's ridiculous that I won't tell you."

Sharley shook her head. "It's more than just ridiculous. You're being hateful and...and offensive!"

His face paled. "Believe me, Sharley, it's for the best."

"And you're the one who decides that? I don't have anything to say about it?"

"I can hardly give you the truth and then ask if you'd rather I take it back and substitute a lie, can I?"

"The truth can't possibly be any worse than this!"

"Yes, it can, Sharley. And once it's said, there's no way to send the truth back into the darkness. Believe me, I'd like to try."

The pain in his voice was undeniable, and it brought a lump to Sharley's throat that was too big to speak around.

Spence let the silence drag out for a moment. "Face it, Sharley, nothing is going to patch this up between us. You can't bring yourself to believe in me, and I...I could never care for a woman who doesn't trust me. Why cause more pain for everyone? Let it go. Just break it off clean. Call it quits. It never happened."

She shook her head, but it was more a gesture of hope-lessness than of disagreement. It's over, she told herself. He's right about that much. Let it go with dignity, Shar-ley. It's the only thing you can do.

"We've made enough mistakes," Spence said quietly. "Why add one more?"

She had to clear her throat twice before she could speak at all, and then her voice was little more than a breath. "I suppose it hardly matters now."

To have let herself hope that anything could be worked out, after all the hurt that had been done to both of them, was just as silly in its own way as believing that Charlotte could have arranged the whole thing just to keep Sharley by her side.

"Exactly." He patted her hand and moved away to the kitchen with her glass.

Sharley sat very still and stared at the back of her hand. Where his fingertips had brushed the soft skin, every cell seemed to quiver with electricity. He had intended it to be a reassuring gesture, Sharley was sure, but instead, it had made her feel incredibly sad.

SHARLEY STIRRED FITFULLY as she drifted back toward consciousness, aware only that she felt terrible. She wanted Libby, she thought. Not Charlotte; despite her own ill-nesses, or perhaps because of them, Charlotte was no use at all in a sickroom. But the Hudsons' housekeeper knew what to do. She understood how much better it felt just to have a cool pillowcase and fresh pajamas.

Yes, it was a good thing Charlotte didn't know that Sharley was up here in the woods, alone—or as good as alone—and ill....

Sharley frowned as she tried to follow that line of thought all the way through. Precisely why shouldn't

Charlotte know? She would be concerned, of course, and it wasn't good for her to worry. But still, Sharley was a grown woman. She had a right to be ill if she wanted.

She tried to smile at the sheer ridiculousness of that thought. Maybe Spence had a point about Charlotte; it was true she was a bit possessive and overprotective. But no one could argue that Charlotte had anything but the best of motives. She did what she thought was right, as anyone did. If keeping Sharley busy helped her get through this crisis, Charlotte was to be thanked. And of course she wanted Sharley to be nearby. Her niece was the only thing Charlotte had—along with Martin, of course. No, Spence was just being too rough on her, blaming poor Charlotte when none of this was her fault at all. . . .

Sharley drifted off to sleep again.

She didn't know how much later it was when she roused to see a dim figure bending over her. His hands clutched her shoulders, and he was administering a shaking so rough she felt as if fireworks were going off inside her brain. In sheer terror, she uttered a strangled little scream.

"Thank God," a hoarse voice said. "You're awake."

Sharley squinted at him. It was almost dark, and her vision was a little blurry. "Congratulations, Spence." Her voice slurred oddly.

"I couldn't rouse you," he said harshly. "I was trying to wake you to see what you wanted for dinner."

The mere thought of food made her feel like retching. "Don't want . . . anything. I'm sick."

"I know you're sick. I didn't realize before just how sick you are. Come on, Sharley. Get up."

"I've got the flu. Let me . . . rest."

"No. It's not flu, Sharley."

She frowned. "My . . . fall?"

"Your fault? What do you... Dammit, it doesn't matter right now. I can't think straight enough to argue with you. We've got to get out of here. It's carbon monoxide, Sharley."

She knew that what he had said should be important to her, but she couldn't for the life of her remember why. Carbon monoxide... She'd simply have to lie still and think about it. Maybe she'd remember when her head stopped pounding.

Spence's voice had a harsh edge to it. "Listen, if I have to, I *will* drag you by the hair. Dammit, Sharley, you have to help. I can't carry you!"

That stung her pride a bit. "I'm not that... fat," she protested weakly.

It was bitterly cold in the cabin. She looked around groggily. Both the doors were open, she realized. And it looked as if someone had taken a hammer to the closest window, too.

"Spence," she said with what little dignity she could muster. "Martin isn't going to like what you've done to his cabin."

"Damn Martin and damn his cabin. You're not getting enough oxygen to your brain. What would you suggest I do? Fan you with a newspaper?" He pulled her to her feet.

She was too dizzy to keep her balance, and Spence practically dragged her to the door. She balked at stepping onto the icy porch, and despite what he had said about not being able to carry her, he simply picked her up. "Don't wriggle," he ordered, and strode the few yards to her car.

Sharley puzzled over that. She had just figured out that if she shifted her weight she might throw him off balance on the ice when he dumped her unceremoniously into the passenger seat. He left the door open and turned back toward the house.

Sharley leaned out, clutching the edge of the seat as best she could to maintain her balance. The world seemed to have started rotating faster. "Where are you going?"

"Back for the ashes I cleaned out of the fireplace."

"But why do you want to take—"

"I'm going to dump them on this slope. With a little extra traction, we might get the car out of here."

Sharley frowned. "Now that we're out of the cabin, it's all right, isn't it?"

"Not quite that simple, darling. You need medical treatment." He leaned over her for a moment, pushing her hair back from her forehead. The warm brush of his fingers felt good against her face.

She supposed he was right, though she didn't seem to be able to think it all the way through for herself. What was happening to her brain, anyway? Everything was still obviously working in Spence's head, so why couldn't *she* function?

"Don't forget how to breathe," he ordered gruffly.

Sharley didn't know how long it was before he came back, shut her door and slid behind the wheel. She noticed with detached interest that though his hands were covered with ash, his knuckles looked white as he turned the ignition key.

"What about you?" she managed. "You were in there, too."

"I'm okay. I wasn't in it as long as you were."

The engine whined for a moment before roaring to life. She saw Spence close his eyes for a second as if in gratitude.

"You mean because you were carrying wood this afternoon while I cleaned?"

"Exactly." He took a deep breath. "Here we go. Say a prayer, sweetheart."

Obediently, Sharley began to chant, "Now I lay me down to sleep, I ask the—"

"Not that one, dammit," Spence said sharply. "Please, not that one!"

She didn't quite understand, but before she could ask him to explain, he had put the car into gear and gently hit the gas. Almost instantly it skidded sideways on the hillside, and Sharley swayed wildly in her seat. "Whee," she said. "It's just like a roller coaster."

"Yeah. You just keep enjoying the ride." The momentum was slowing as the tires grabbed for traction on the ice, and Spence tried to steer the car back onto the ash-covered path. They eased over the hill with the last tiny bit of forward motion.

"You did it," Sharley said exultantly.

"Only the first obstacle of many, I'm afraid." The driveway sloped down toward the road, and the car began picking up speed. Spence carefully applied the brake, but to little avail. "Hang on," he ordered, and the car skidded around and onto the road with an ominous thump. "Sorry about that. But keeping three wheels on the road, in these conditions, isn't a bad record at all." He looked ahead at the next hill and sighed.

Sharley yawned.

"Don't start that," Spence warned. "Please, just do your best to stay awake, Sharley. Dammit, I should have known something wasn't right. The stuffy smell... I thought the place was just stale and dirty from being closed up so long. And all the condensation on the windows should have made me suspicious, too. There was enough humidity in the air to make the drawers stick. That shouldn't happen in this weather—you were right."

"I was?" Even though she was shivering from the cold, Sharley was still feeling sleepy.

"Absolutely. When fuel doesn't burn completely, it gives off moisture, as well as toxic gases. It's one of the classic signs—one of the only signs, since you can't smell carbon monoxide itself. But I was so convinced the cabin was full of holes that it never occurred to me to look for the obvious."

"What was it?" Sharley managed. "That poisoned us, I mean. The fireplace?"

"I don't know. A cracked chimney could have let the gases seep back into the cabin, or a plugged vent on the kitchen range. Maybe a squirrel built a nest on top of the stovepipe. I wasn't going to stick around and look."

With agonizing slowness the car crept toward the ridge of the hill. Sometimes it seemed to move as many feet sideways as forward, but Spence steered cautiously and did not take his foot off the gas pedal. Eventually they crept over the top.

"Why wouldn't Martin have noticed something wrong?" Sharley asked.

"Maybe there wasn't anything to notice last time he was here. It's been a year at least, hasn't it?"

Sharley nodded, but he hadn't taken his eyes off the road. "I suppose so."

"And there wasn't any reason for the caretaker to give the place a careful going-over, because he didn't expect it to be used this winter. It was careless of him not to have taken a look when Martin called him, of course. But he probably thought the same thing I did—that the place was so leaky there could never be a problem with getting enough fresh air."

Sharley looked at the next hill. It was higher than the one they had just managed, and halfway up, a fallen tree limb partially blocked the road. She closed her eyes and thought, Spence will handle it.

"I wonder if the ice is what sealed it up tight," Spence mused. "Sort of like wrapping a plastic bag around the whole building. And the longer we stayed inside..." He turned his head sharply. "Keep talking to me, dammit," he ordered. "Don't cash in on me now, Sharley. Stay with me..."

The car skidded the instant his attention was distracted, and he fought to get it back under control. Sharley opened her eyes and watched with mild interest. The roadside ditch seemed to be coming closer each time the car swung.

They missed the ditch by the width of a feather, but all their momentum was lost, so Spence had to back down the hill to make another run. That was the worst of it, though, and a few minutes later Sharley pointed at a house, little more than a dark shadow beside the road. "There's where Joe Baxter lives."

Spence grunted as he maneuvered the car off the road and into the narrow gravel drive. His hand was trembling as he shut the engine off. "Looks as if there's no power here, either. Sit still." He left his car door open and strode toward the house.

Sharley wanted to complain about the draft, but she didn't have the energy. She began to slowly extract herself from the car, instead. Her muscles were working a little better, but not much.

She heard Spence pounding on the door and saw it open. A grizzly bear of a man leaned out.

Spence said sharply, "I need to get Miss Collins to a hospital."

"Sharley? Sure, come on in and we'll call for an ambulance."

"Can an ambulance get here?"

As she stumbled toward the house, Sharley listened with detached interest. An ambulance? For her? She'd never been sick enough to need an ambulance in her life. She started to protest.

Spence wheeled around. "I told you to sit still!"

"I was cold," she complained.

He scooped her up in his arms. Joe Baxter held the door wide.

"Your telephone actually works?" Spence said as he put Sharley down on a long couch near the front door.

"Nope. It's out because of the ice. Got a CB, though. What's the problem?"

Sharley could see relief washing across Spence's face. He sat down abruptly on a big hassock nearby and dropped his face into his hands as he told Joe Baxter what had happened at the cabin.

Joe's jaw tightened, but he didn't say a word. He vanished toward the back of the house.

Sharley groped for Spence's hand, but she couldn't reach it, and she was too exhausted to sit up. "It'll be all right now," she murmured.

He wet his lips and tried to smile. "Yeah. It'll be all right. As soon as the ambulance gets here."

That would be a relief, she thought. She wasn't feeling much better, after all. She nodded and put her head down.

The couch was right next to a big old-fashioned wood stove, and Sharley soon stopped shivering and drifted off again, not into true sleep but a state of half-awareness. She vaguely heard Joe Baxter say the ambulance was on its way, but she didn't really pay attention; it was too much effort. And though she expected Spence to fuss at her for not staying alert, he didn't.

Even the bustle of the paramedics only partially aroused her. She was aware, in a detached way, of them checking her blood pressure and taking her pulse. And she knew perfectly well when they strapped the mask on her face, for it made her feel as if she was smothering, and she fought it until the cool flow of oxygen began to soothe her tormented lungs. She hadn't realized how much it hurt to breathe, until the pain diminished.

"Lucky you guys were in the area," Joe Baxter said.

The paramedic who was bending over Sharley muttered, "You can say that again."

She looked up at Spence, her eyes widening in horror as she realized for the first time just how serious this was.

He brushed the hair back off her face, away from the mask. "You'll be fine now, Sharley. They'll take good care of you."

And then, as Sharley watched, unable to move, unable to help, Spence—like a puppet whose strings have been cut—simply folded up and slid to the floor.

CHAPTER EIGHT

SHARLEY SAT UP, her head swimming with shock and confusion. The paramedic who was working on her put one hand on her shoulder and pushed her down on the stretcher. It was almost a reflex action; he didn't even turn his head toward the flurry of activity behind him as the other two paramedics converged on Spence.

"Was he in the cabin, too?" he asked Sharley.

Her voice was muffled by the oxygen mask, and she had to make a great effort to enunciate. "Yes. He got me out. Carried me to the car."

"*Carried* you? Dammit. And of course the fool didn't say anything." He called over his shoulder, "You've got exertion on top of probable carbon monoxide there."

"He'll be all right, won't he?" Sharley managed.

"Sure he will. Settle down now and just concentrate on breathing as slowly and deeply as you can."

But he was not telling the truth; he was not certain Spence would be all right. Sharley knew that in her bones, and the certainty cleared her mind as nothing else could have. "He hurt himself trying to save me, didn't he?"

The paramedic looked directly at her for an instant. "It didn't do him any good," he admitted. "But he's a whole lot bigger than you. He's got more blood volume, so he can take more than you can."

But not that much more, Sharley thought. Even though Spence had been outside for part of the afternoon, he'd been breathing the same poisoned air she had for hours, and like her, slowly growing weaker. No wonder he'd said he couldn't carry her.

And then he'd gone ahead and done it, anyway, she remembered. While she had been too far out of her mind even to know what was going on, Spence had managed to hold himself together, get both of them to help and save their lives....

At least, she hoped he had managed to save them both.

It must have been sheer adrenaline that had kept him going, so it wasn't so surprising that the instant the pressure was off, he had collapsed. If the stress, on top of the carbon monoxide, was what had knocked him out, then he would be all right—wouldn't he?

She could twist her head around just far enough to see him from the corner of her eye. His face was flushed and expressionless under the oxygen mask, and his eyes were closed. She watched as they lifted him onto a stretcher; his body was limp.

One of the other paramedics said, "All right, we're ready to transport," and the one bending over Sharley tucked the blanket more tightly around her and checked the straps that held her to the stretcher. Joe Baxter helped to carry her outside.

It wasn't a normal ambulance that waited in the roadway, but a helicopter, with engines throbbing and warning lights blinking steadily. Painted on its side was the name of the hospital—a large metropolitan care center known for its emergency services.

"A helicopter?" she asked weakly.

The paramedic locked her stretcher in place across from Spence's. "Yeah. Since the rural roads are still a mess, we got called in to do a routine transport that a ground crew would normally handle. So we were already at the local hospital when they diverted us to pick you up.''

He's talking to distract me, she thought, and to reassure me—telling me, whether it's true or not, that Spence really isn't in such serious condition, after all.

She looked over at the other stretcher. ''I'm glad you were here,'' she whispered.

The helicopter lifted off. It felt to Sharley as if it was rocking wildly, or perhaps that was only because her head was still aching. The pain wasn't nearly as bad as it had been, though, and on the whole, she was feeling much more like her normal self—except when she caught a glimpse of Spence.

I'm safe, she thought. But what about him? He risked his life for me, and I can't even thank him or tell him it will be all right.

She closed her eyes, and the words of the childhood prayer she had begun to chant earlier came to her mind once more. ''Now I lay me down to sleep...'' Spence had snapped at her for saying it, and her mind had been so fogged she hadn't understood why. Now she knew: The little rhyme went on, ''If I should die before I wake...''

No, she thought fiercely. *They won't let that happen. Not to Spence.*

IN THE EMERGENCY ROOM of the hospital, it might as well have been high noon, instead of— What time was it, anyway? Sharley hadn't the vaguest idea. It had been dark when Spence had roused her in the cabin. But how long had it taken them to get to the Baxters' house? How long had they waited for the helicopter?

Trying to figure it out only made her head hurt worse, so she closed her eyes and lay passively as they worked on her, terribly conscious that in another curtained cubicle nearby Spence lay, probably still unaware of the frantic bustle around him. He hadn't even moved as they took the stretcher off the helicopter and wheeled it into the hospital. Shouldn't the oxygen have had some effect by now?

If only she hadn't gone to the cabin at all, she thought, none of this would have happened. Or at least Spence wouldn't have exhausted himself in trying to save her, and he'd be all right—

No. It was more likely he'd be dead. The difficulty of rousing her had warned him; if she hadn't been there, he might not have realized in time. In any case, there was no point in wishing things undone now.

And if she had the power to turn back the clock and do things differently, she wouldn't begin with the cabin. She'd go farther back, to that Friday afternoon when she had come home from school and gone straight to the gardener's cottage—and she would turn away at the front door and walk to the main house, instead. Since she wouldn't have known anything about Wendy, the wedding would have come off on schedule, and she and Spence would be honeymooning in the Bahamas this week, not gasping for breath in the hospital.

For a moment, she lost herself in the daydream of sun and sand, perfect harmony, laughter and love. If only she hadn't walked into the cottage and seen him there with Wendy...

Sharley crashed back to reality, horrified at how sensible that scenario seemed. What an ostrich you are, she told herself, pretending danger doesn't exist if you can't see it! Would she really rather have remained ignorant of Wendy? Even if he had broken off that particular affair completely, it didn't mean everything would be rosy from then on. A man who wasn't faithful to his fiancée wasn't likely to be faithful to his wife, either—no matter how good his intentions. Wendy wouldn't be the last...

It isn't what you think, he had said.

Was it conceivable he was telling the truth? And if Sharley's interpretation of the incident in the cottage was wrong, what was the truth?

You either believe in him or you don't, Sharley reminded herself. There was no halfway measure. She either loved him for what he was, or else she had to admit she'd never truly known him at all.

And what about Spence? Did he love Sharley and treasure her—or was she only a means to an end?

Tonight in the cabin, he must have realized he was at risk, too, and that every bit of exertion increased the danger. But he had worked frantically, without thought for himself, to get her to safety. And the moment Sharley was being taken care of he had collapsed, as if his job was done and he no longer cared about anything else.

I *do* mean something to him, she thought. No one would have blamed him if he'd simply dragged me outside into the fresh air and let me take my chances alongside him. If he's sacrificed himself to save me—

''We're going to move you to another room now,'' one of the nurses told her. Sharley hardly heard.

If only I could tell him I understand, she thought.

In the wide hallway, the orderly pushing her stretcher paused to let another patient be moved. Sharley, watching idly, saw a thatch of rumpled dark hair—

''Spence!'' she said, and tried to put her hand out to stop the orderlies who were moving him. It would have been an imperious gesture, like a queen issuing orders to the royal bearers, except that Sharley had forgotten they'd strapped her in.

So the best she could do was look at him as the stretcher slid by. He turned his head, and she saw that his eyes were open. Even though they seemed glazed, with none of their usual brilliance, she gave a tiny sob of relief. He was awake, at least. That was enough to give her hope.

His forehead wrinkled a little, and he said something. The oxygen mask he wore made it difficult to hear, but Sharley could have sworn he said, "It wasn't me."

Then he was gone. She had not been able to touch him, or tell him that she appreciated what he had done, or even whisper that she loved him.

There will be time later for that, she told herself. I'm sure of it.

It wasn't me, he'd said. What on earth could he mean?

MARTIN REACHED the hospital in the small hours of the morning. Sharley happened to be awake having her vital signs checked and another vial of blood drawn, so the nurse let him come in for a few minutes. He stood quietly beside the bed, just looking at her.

She blinked at him in surprise. "How did you get here?"

"Joe Baxter got a message to me. I phoned the hospital right away, and they said you were doing fine, but..." Even in the dim light she could see the shine of tears in his eyes.

Sharley didn't think she could handle it if Martin broke down. "I meant the ice and everything."

"Oh. The main highways are in fairly good condition now. It's only the side roads that are still bad."

"So you drove up here in the middle of the night?" She let a half-scolding note creep into her voice, and she was rewarded with a tiny smile.

"Had to make sure my girl was all right, didn't I? Sharley, I didn't know what to think when I got Joe's message that you'd been airlifted out of his place. I thought it was just a garbled-up thirdhand report—that Spence had an accident and somebody got confused. Then when I found out it really was you, even though I had no idea you were at the cabin in the first place..."

"I'm sorry about that, Uncle Martin." Sharley pushed the button that raised the head of the bed. "I should have told you I wasn't going to the resort."

"Would have saved a bit of trouble, I'd say." He gave her a sidelong glance. "Or did you and Spence get things straightened out?"

"You never stop hoping, do you, Uncle Martin?" She reached for the glass of ice water on her bedside table. "No, we didn't. Have you seen him?"

"Not yet." He held the glass while she pulled the oxygen mask away from her face for a moment.

The cold water tasted good, and Sharley took a long drink. "Is Charlotte upset with me?"

"For vanishing like that? I don't know that I'd call her upset. She's worried, of course."

"She didn't come with you, did she?"

Martin shook his head. "She thought she'd better not risk going out till daylight, so Libby will bring her up."

"That's good." Sharley rearranged the mask and settled back against her pillows. "There isn't any sense in her sitting here at all hours, anyway."

"Sharley, I'm so awfully sorry." Martin twisted the brim of his hat between his hands. "It's my fault. All of it. I've caused you nothing but trouble, my dear...." His voice trembled, and for the first time Sharley could remember, he looked every year of his age.

She patted his sleeve reassuringly. "It was an accident. You mustn't blame yourself."

The nurse leaned in. "I think that's long enough, Mr. Hudson. Miss Collins needs her rest."

"And so do you, Uncle Martin. I'll see you in the morning."

He gave her a long sad look, as if he was memorizing every inch of her face, then nodded and turned toward the door.

The nurse added, "I checked on Mr. Greenfield's condition, Mr. Hudson. He's doing much better after his hyperbaric oxygen treatment, but he's still in the intensive-care unit, and the doctor says no visitors until tomorrow at least."

Sharley sat up. "Hyper— What's that?"

"Oxygen under pressure." The nurse's tone was warm and reassuring. "It's a fairly standard treatment to force the carbon monoxide out of the blood faster. Now, you just relax and get some sleep."

Sharley bit her lip and sagged against her pillows. Cut it out, she told herself. She had known in her heart Spence was far worse off than she was, because he had taken so long to wake up. But having her intuition confirmed by a medical authority gave the fact an uncomfortable reality.

She lay there quietly, more wide awake than she had been in almost a full day. In the distance she could hear the wail of a siren as an ambulance delivered a patient to the emergency room far below her window.

Spence was doing much better now. She would hang on to that knowledge. And tomorrow, when he was allowed visitors, she would go and see him, thank him for saving her life, and ask him what he had meant by those few words in the emergency-room hallway.

It wasn't me. Had he been talking about the scene at the gardener's cottage? But that was ridiculous. It was impossible that she could have been mistaken; she had been in the same room. Had spoken to him.

What was he asking her to believe? That she'd been hallucinating when she saw him with Wendy in his arms? Or that he had a double hidden away somewhere, a twin that no one in Hammond's Point had ever heard of?

You're having delusions now, Sharley told herself, going to these lengths to try to find an explanation! Maybe he was talking about something else altogether.

She would simply wait till morning, and as soon as her doctor checked her over and released her, she would go and confront Spence.

BUT MORNING DID NOT BRING what Sharley had expected. Instead of having a simple, cheerful chat with her doctor, followed by instructions for her home care and orders for her release, she was wheeled down to the neurological department for what the doctor called a complete battery of tests.

"Whenever a person is subjected to oxygen starvation," he explained, "there's a possibility of long-term neurological damage. I believe in your case the risk is remote, since you responded so promptly to treatment, but it makes no sense to take chances."

Sharley couldn't disagree with that, but by the time they brought her back to her room for lunch she couldn't help wishing she'd been left alone to recuperate. She was a great deal weaker than she'd expected to be, and all she wanted was a few spoonfuls of soup, a drink of water and a blissfully dark and quiet room for the rest of the day.

"Now I know why he called it a battery of tests," she told the nurse's aide who helped her back into bed. "Except that 'assault and battery' would have been a better description. My whole body feels as if it's been beaten."

The aide smiled. "That's why he didn't order all the tests for today." She pushed the lunch tray into place and handed Sharley a spoon.

"There are *more*?" Sharley wailed.

The door opened and Charlotte Hudson swept in, her ebony walking stick clicking against the tile floor. "My dear!" she exclaimed. "What a terrible fright you've given us!"

Sharley sighed and started to stir her chicken soup. "I know, Aunt Charlotte, and I'm sorry."

"To find that you weren't at the resort at all was a shock in itself. Fortunately I hadn't tried to call you earlier. I hate to think what state of mind I'd have been in when I found you missing. Then this happens..." She fanned herself with her gloves. "It was nearly too much. You look quite dreadful, dear."

Libby said, "She looks better than she has any right to, everything considered."

"The oxygen mask has left terrible red creases on your face," Charlotte said fretfully.

"They'll go away." Libby took off her hat and draped her coat over the back of a chair. "If you're only going to play with that soup, Sharley, I'll feed you. I've done it a good many times before."

"I can feed myself," Sharley said. But she didn't argue when Libby moved to the side of the bed and took the soup spoon. Obediently she opened her mouth for the first spoonful.

"And she doesn't need any lectures just now, either," Libby told Charlotte. "Let her get home at least before you start in on her about being a thoughtless and ungrateful child." She winked at Sharley.

Charlotte said, "I had no intention of telling her anything of the sort. I simply informed her of how terribly
upset Martin and I were when we heard the news."

"Same thing," Libby muttered under her breath.

Between the two of them and the soup, Sharley knew she
wouldn't have a chance to speak, so she didn't even try.

"But at least you won't have lasting effects," Charlotte
announced.

Sharley frowned. Had she put just a tiny bit of emphasis on the pronoun? She shook her head at the next
spoonful of soup. "What about Spence? Is he worse this
morning?"

Charlotte's carefully plucked eyebrows rose just a little.
"I don't know, and I don't care to make any effort to find
out."

Martin tapped on the half-open door and came in.
"He's better. I just saw him." There was a quiet note of
authority in his voice, and Sharley relaxed a little.

"Before you even came to see Sharley?" Charlotte
snapped.

Martin ignored her. He came up to the side of Sharley's
bed and clasped his hands on the rail. "How are you this
morning?"

"So far it appears I still have a whole brain." She saw
the shadow in his eyes and regretted the flippant answer.
"I'm fine, Uncle Martin." She reached for his hand. "Is
Spence really all right?"

"I think so. They've still got a No Visitors sign on the
door, but the nurse let me go in for a minute." Martin
looked down at her slim fingers, pale against the brown of
his skin. "I've talked to Joe Baxter, too. He went over to
the cabin first thing this morning. The vent pipe on the
water heater was blocked by a bunch of twigs. Some bird
had worked awfully hard to push those sticks down into

the pipe, trying to build a nest. Joe said the blockage was completely out of sight.''

"So the exhaust spilled back into the cabin,'' Sharley said. To think she and Spence had both been so grateful to have hot water after the power went out—and it had almost killed them. "I'm glad to know what it was. Such a simple thing to cause all this trouble, isn't it?''

Charlotte gave a ladylike snort. "Well, there won't be any more trouble of that kind.''

"Of course not,'' Martin said. He sounded surprised. "Joe took care of the nest before he even called me. But just in case it wasn't the only problem, there will be a full inspection before anyone spends even an hour in that cabin again.''

"I was thinking more in terms of selling the place,'' Charlotte said.

"Oh, Aunt Charlotte—''

"It's an awful shack, filthy and smelly and unpleasant. I never understood your fondness for it, Martin. Besides, I can't believe you could ever bring yourself to go up there again, knowing it almost cost Sharley's life.''

"It's not Uncle Martin's fault,'' Sharley protested. "It wouldn't be fair to make him give up the cabin.''

"It's ridiculous to keep it,'' Charlotte said mulishly.

Martin squeezed Sharley's hand. "Don't fret,'' he said softly. "That's the least of my worries right now.'' He turned to Charlotte. "You're upsetting Sharley with this nonsense.''

"Nonsense? Is that what you call my honest concern? And who, I ask you, is the cause of her being here in the first place?''

"Stop it,'' Sharley said. Her voice was trembling. "Please, both of you, go home. I just want to sleep.''

The ensuing silence seemed to drag out for hours before Charlotte stood up. "Very well," she said crisply. "Come along, Martin. I believe we've been dismissed."

Martin clung to Sharley's hand for an instant longer. "I'll talk to you later, honey."

She smiled at him, grateful that he, at least, seemed to understand.

Libby patted Sharley's shoulder. "I'll do my best to keep them away for a day or two," she promised. "Though I don't make any guarantees."

But even in the peaceful quiet of Sharley's room, sleep didn't come easily. The soft hiss of the oxygen lines and the small noises from the hallway—voices and soft-soled shoes and equipment carts going back and forth—reminded her that down the hall somewhere Spence was going through the same things she was.

Martin had told her Spence was better today. But there had been something about the way he'd said it that made her wonder just a little. She wished she could go and see for herself.

It was wrong to keep her in the dark about his condition; if things had been oh-so-slightly different, the doctors would have been making special efforts to give her every detail. They wouldn't have been able to keep her away from him, either; no matter how few visitors were allowed, wives were never turned away.

That was what she wanted.

There are certain conditions, she reminded herself. Could she accept them?

Could she honestly tell herself that she believed in Spence's innocence? Despite the fact that there seemed to be no explanation on earth that made sense, could she take his word that nothing had happened in the gardener's cottage?

And no matter what had been between him and Wendy, or whether she ever knew, could she honestly put it behind her? Not only forgive, but forget?

If I only knew he loved me, she thought, I believe I could.

But she did know that. Surely what he had done last night had proved it. He had nearly sacrificed himself to save her life, and if that wasn't love, what was?

As soon as she had the chance, she decided, she would tell him that explanations didn't matter anymore, that his word was enough. And she would ask him if they couldn't start all over again.

As soon as she had the strength.

TWO MORE FULL DAYS passed before her doctor agreed that it was safe for her to go home. "But no school for at least another week," he decreed. "Get some exercise, but take it easy—slow walks, not racquetball. I'll want to see you again before I let you go back to full activity."

Sharley nodded.

"Don't worry, Doctor," Charlotte said. "We'll watch our little invalid very closely. I certainly know the danger involved in doing too much too soon." She patted Sharley's arm. "Get your coat on now, dear, and Libby and I will take you home."

Sharley obediently slipped her down-filled coat over the elegant trouser suit Charlotte had brought. What was the woman thinking of, she wondered, when she had picked out that particular outfit? Jeans would have been much more comfortable on the long ride ahead. "I wish Martin could have come with you."

Charlotte said briskly, "He wanted to, but he had business to attend to. With Spence unavailable, everything has fallen on Martin's shoulders."

"Of course I understand." But Sharley missed him, nevertheless. Martin had come back to visit her only once, and even then Charlotte had been with him. She hadn't had another chance to ask about the cabin, her car—or Spence.

Sharley looked down the hall toward Spence's room. The door was shut, and the No Visitors sign was still up. Sharley was certain it no longer meant guests weren't allowed for medical reasons, but that they weren't wanted at all, and yesterday she had walked up and down this hall a half-dozen times, trying to find the courage to violate the order and knock on the door.

One of the nurses approached. "It's awfully nice to see you up and dressed and ready to leave us," she said. "We'll miss you—and Mr. Greenfield, too."

"Is he going home today, too?" Sharley tried to keep her voice casual.

"Another day or two probably. Why don't you step in and say goodbye? I'm sure he'd like to see you."

"But the sign . . ."

"Oh, that. He said it can come down today."

She was referring to Spence, Sharley thought, not his doctor. And he meant the sign to stay up until Sharley had gone, no doubt. She started to shake her head.

But the nurse had already crossed the hall to tap on the door. "There's a young lady here to see you," she said cheerfully, and gestured to Sharley.

She wet her lips nervously. "I'll be just a minute, Aunt Charlotte."

All she could see at first was a silhouette; Spence was sitting in an armchair with his back to the window. Then, as Sharley's eyes adjusted, she drank in the sight of him—clean shaven again, wearing hospital-issue pajamas and a bright plaid bathrobe. He seemed a little pale, and his mouth was set tightly. But on the whole he looked wonderful.

What would happen if I ran to him? Sharley wondered. If I threw myself in his arms, or knelt beside his chair...

"I'll leave you," a woman's voice said.

A nurse, Sharley thought. But she knew better, even before she turned around. There was no mistaking that soft voice. What was Wendy Taylor doing here now? If Spence wasn't being released for a day or two, she hadn't come to drive him back to Hammond's Point.

Don't be stupid, Sharley told herself. She's visiting him, of course. I was right about that sign on the door. It didn't mean no visitors at all, just selected ones.

"Don't go, Wendy," she said. "Charlotte's waiting to take me home. I just came in to say goodbye."

Spence stood up. "It's none of my business, of course, but is she going to make you into an invalid now, too?"

"Spence!" Wendy protested.

Sharley thought the woman sounded as if she was correcting an erring child. What she couldn't believe was the way Spence reacted to the rebuke—with a slight flush and a sidelong glance at Wendy.

He's acting as if he's given her that power over him, Sharley thought incredulously, and her last whisper of hope died painfully. There was nothing else to do but make as graceful an exit as possible.

She tipped up her chin to look at Spence. "You're right," she said coolly. "It's none of your business."

Wendy stirred nervously.

Don't worry, Sharley almost said. *I can't get out of here soon enough.*

But there were a couple of things that still had to be said, no matter how badly her dreams had been smashed. "I never had a chance to thank you, Spence, and tell you that I appreciate everything you did for me. I hope you'll soon be better."

And that was all. She thought she heard him call her name, but the whoosh of the door closing behind her drowned it out. Or perhaps it had only been imagination.

In any case, it no longer mattered.

CHAPTER NINE

SHARLEY STIRRED restlessly on the chaise lounge in the sun room at the back of the Hudson house. It was two o'clock Friday afternoon; right about now, she thought, the substitute teacher should be handing out the math-review work sheet Sharley had left. Then there would be recess, and social studies, and the end of another week.

With March break over, school had started again yesterday, without Sharley. Of course, she reminded herself, if she had to take a few days of sick leave, this was the best possible time, since she'd left everything ready for a substitute, anyway. But that didn't make it any easier to sit idly at home. She felt fine now, after a couple of days out of the hospital. Perhaps she could go back earlier than the doctor had expected.

But if she was honest with herself, she had to admit that missing school wasn't the only thing on her mind. She looked down at the textbook lying open on her knees. She had been staring at the same two pages for almost an hour now and thinking about Spence.

She should be glad she hadn't make a fool of herself in his hospital room. How embarrassing it would have been if she had declared her belief that Wendy meant nothing to him, and then he had to tell her how wrong she was.

For she *had* been wrong about Wendy, that was apparent; the woman was important to him, or she wouldn't have spoken in that scolding way to him, as if she had every right to correct his failings. Spence wouldn't have allowed it.

No, if Wendy wasn't important she wouldn't even have been there in his room at all—

The doorbell chimed, and Sharley closed the textbook on her lap and started to get up. From a deep chair across the sun room, Charlotte said, "Libby will get it."

"Libby has plenty to do. I'm perfectly capable." But before she was on her feet, Sharley heard the housekeeper's footsteps on the slate of the entrance hall. She sank back into the chaise as Libby ushered three of Charlotte's friends into the room.

Just what I need, Sharley thought. A restful afternoon's visit with the bridge ladies.

"Charlotte, what a shock this must have been for you!" one of them twittered as she rushed across the room. "We just had to come to give you some support."

Charlotte sat up straighter. "That's very thoughtful of you. It has been a trial, I must admit. Of course now that Sharley's safely home—"

"I'll leave you to chat," Sharley murmured. She stacked her textbooks and notepads. "I have some studying to do."

"Good heavens," Charlotte said, "that's all you've been doing for two days. You need a change of pace. Libby, bring in the tea tray."

"Oh, yes, do stay, Sharley," another of the ladies said. "Such a dreadful accident. You're awfully lucky to have no lasting effects from it." She gave a little shiver. "You don't...do you?"

"My cousin William had carbon-monoxide poisoning once," the first woman recalled. "He had a heart attack shortly afterward, poor man. He was very young, too—young for a heart attack, at least. His doctor always said it was because that poisoning weakened his system."

Thanks a lot, Sharley thought. That kind of cheerfully told horror story was the last thing she needed to hear. Spence was a young man, too—far too young for a heart attack in the ordinary course of events.

The third woman, who hadn't said a word till then, settled herself in a chair beside Charlotte's. "Personally I find the whole episode distinctly odd."

Sharley raised her eyebrows in what she intended to be a blighting look. "I can't imagine what you mean."

"For one thing, it seems quite strange that Spence was even there at the cabin with you. After the very public way you two split up, it is certainly unusual."

Don't say anything, Sharley warned herself. You'll only make it worse if you try to explain.

"Oh, I think it's so romantic." The woman who had asked about aftereffects patted Sharley's hand. "Is it true that Spence rescued you?"

"Quite true," Sharley admitted.

The woman gave an arch laugh. "Then I suppose there will be another interesting announcement soon?"

"I can't imagine what it would be," Sharley said crisply. She didn't have to put up with this. On the other hand, she couldn't just pick up her books and walk out, either.

"But after he saved your life, my dear, surely you can find it in your heart—"

"Don't be silly," Charlotte said. "Spence did what anyone would, and it certainly doesn't change the facts. Now, this whole thing makes me quite nervous, so shall we talk of something else?"

Sharley tried to hide her sigh of relief.

Charlotte turned to the woman sitting beside her. "I was going to call you about your reception on Monday," she confided. "I'm afraid I can't come, after all. The stress of this week has been too much for me."

"But Charlotte, you promised to pour tea! And it's such a special event you simply can't miss it. It isn't every day that Hammond's Point gets to hear such a famous musician. And to be able to actually talk to him after his recital will be a real treat!"

"Yes, I know, and I deeply regret not getting to meet him. But I'm sure Sharley will be happy to take my place and pour for you."

Sharley slowly turned her head to study her aunt. What was it Spence had said about Charlotte's activities and the way she casually passed on to Sharley anything she didn't want to do? Not that Spence's opinions about anything mattered to her anymore. Still, the last thing she would feel like doing on Monday evening was pouring tea.

"Aunt Charlotte," she said, "I don't think I can."

"Nonsense, dear. It's just a little reception. It will do you good to get out and have something to occupy your mind for an hour or two."

"But I'm planning to go to school Monday, and I think I should have a quiet evening after my first day back on the job."

Charlotte sounded horrified. "The doctor said no school for at least a week, Sharley!"

"I know he did. But I'm feeling quite fit again now, and by Monday I'm sure I'll be fine. Why shouldn't I go?" Sharley was starting to feel rebellious. "You said yourself that it will do me good to get out and have something to occupy my mind."

"The reception is a different sort of thing altogether," Charlotte said. "You're certainly not up to running after little hoodlums on a playground."

Sharley shrugged. "I'll swap playground duty with the other teachers for another week or so, and I'll get an aide to help out with any strenuous stuff in the classroom." The idea was becoming more inviting as she worked it out. "As a matter of fact, I think I'll take care of some loose ends today, so I'll be ready when Monday comes." She gathered up her books. "If you will excuse me... Do you have anything that needs to go to the cleaners, Aunt Charlotte?"

"If I did," Charlotte said coldly, "I would not tear myself away from my guests to find it."

"Of course not," Sharley murmured. "I wouldn't expect you to leave your friends. Good afternoon, ladies."

As she climbed the two steps to the bedroom wing, her attitude was lighter than it had been in a couple of weeks. She would look forward, she told herself firmly, and quit dwelling on the past. Progress was made up of small steps, and it was time to begin taking some of them.

She gathered up two suits, a pair of wool trousers and a half-dozen sweaters and poked them into a shopping bag. She'd pick up a couple of her winter coats on her way out, too; the calendar said spring had arrived, and surely warm weather wasn't far away.

I've made a start, she thought. A positive attitude—that was the key.

From the window she caught a glimpse of Martin, puttering around the flower beds at the side of the house. He saw her, too, and waved; in fact, he beckoned at her to come out.

Just what I need on top of the bridge ladies, Sharley thought. Another pep talk from Martin! He couldn't seem to realize that nothing had changed, and that nothing was going to change, either. Last night at dinner, in fact, he'd carried on about Spence until Charlotte had finally snapped at him.

But after Sharley put the shopping bag in the back of her car, she strolled around the house to meet him. It wasn't

Martin's fault that he didn't know when to give up, at least where Spence was concerned. There was something about that bulldog loyalty of his that was touching.

If I'd had that same kind of attitude all along, Sharley thought, things might have turned out differently.

But not for long. Wendy would still have been there, right between us....

Martin must have left the office very early, she thought, for he had changed into his gardening clothes, and one of the flower beds bore evidence of extensive work. But she wouldn't have known he was home at all if she hadn't happened to look out her window. Sharley wondered if he and Libby had some sort of pact of secrecy; he certainly hadn't set foot in the main part of the house this afternoon.

"I haven't had a chance to really talk to you since you got home, Sharley."

His tone was almost accusing, she thought. "I've been right here in the house the whole time, Uncle Martin."

"I know. But Charlotte's always got you close." He pulled off his gloves and tugged his gardening hat down tighter over his ears. "I haven't been able to get a single word with you."

Sharley frowned. "I know she's been a bit overanxious, but—"

"Come and sit with me for a little while, all right?" He led the way to a bench at the edge of the rose garden. Sharley sat down; Martin picked out a nearby bit of grass and started wiping the mud off his shoes. He wasn't looking at her.

"Uncle Martin, I wish you'd stop behaving like a spy."

He didn't smile. "This isn't going to be easy, Sharley. It's not pleasant for me, and it's going to be a shock to you. But it's got to be said."

The note of doom in his voice twisted Sharley's heart like a wet sponge. She tried to swallow the lump in her throat. "It's Spence, isn't it?"

"In a manner of speaking, yes."

Sharley's hands clenched together till her knuckles ached. "He's not going to snap back from the carbon monoxide, is he? That's why they kept him in the hospital—"

"No! He's fine, that way. As a matter of fact, he's back in the office this afternoon, just for a couple of hours. That's why I could sneak out and try to talk to you."

She had to make a physical effort to unlock her hands. "Then...if it's not Spence's health, what is this about?"

His voice was very low. "I'm a coward, Sharley. A rotten, stinking coward. But last week when I thought you were going to die, and it was my fault—"

"It wasn't," she protested automatically.

"It brought me to my senses real fast. I tried to tell you that first night in the hospital, before the nurse shooed me away. Well, that's all right—you were pretty weak just then. But ever since, I haven't had a chance to get a word with you. Charlotte's kept you right beside her."

"Uncle Martin..."

He took a deep breath and turned to face her. Sharley saw the pain in his eyes. "It wasn't Spence in the cottage that day with Wendy."

One endless moment passed, and Sharley started to laugh, almost hysterically. "What do you mean? Of course it was Spence. I saw him. I talked to him!"

"Yes, you saw him. But it wasn't what you thought." He took a deep breath. "Wendy and Spence aren't having an affair, Sharley. They never were. She was there to meet me."

THE WHOLE WORLD turned a peculiar shade of pea green, and Sharley had to hang on to the edge of the bench to keep herself upright. She barely heard what Martin was saying; his words seemed to slide off the edges of her mind like water overflowing a container.

"It's been about a year, I suppose, since we started our affair." Martin sighed. "I never intended to get involved with another woman...."

Sharley's voice felt raspy in her throat, as if she hadn't used it in a hundred years. "No one ever does, Uncle Martin."

"I suppose you're right. But Wendy is sweet and good and lovable and—"

"All the things Charlotte isn't?"

Martin looked at her sharply. "Charlotte has her short-comings," he said quietly. "In the last few years, since her stroke... Well, she's certainly not the woman she used to be."

Sharley nodded.

"That doesn't excuse my behavior, of course, and I don't mean to blame Charlotte for what I did. I'm a married man having an affair, and that's all there is to say about it. Not very pretty, is it?"

Sharley just looked at him.

Martin sighed. "At any rate, we used the cottage because—"

"Right under Charlotte's nose?"

"Er, yes. It was handy."

"I'll bet," she murmured.

"Wendy had a key, and as Spence's secretary she had a good excuse for being at the cottage, so we were far less likely to be noticed here than at a hotel, or even her apartment."

"I suppose you're right. I wouldn't have thought of it myself." Sharley was almost shaking with anger. "But my honeymoon cottage, Uncle Martin—how could you?"

It was obvious he heard the pain in her voice. "Sharley, sweetheart, I'm sorry. It was unforgivable of me. It wouldn't have continued. . . ."

"Is that supposed to make me feel better?"

"My only explanation is that I'd blinded myself to the implications of what I was doing." Martin's voice was soft, but there was an undeniable dignity about it. "I suppose I thought that if I never considered the consequences we'd face if we were discovered, it would never happen, and so I continued to take ridiculous risks."

Sharley dug into her coat pocket for a tissue. "And you were caught."

"Yes. Spence walked in on Wendy in the cottage, and of course he demanded an explanation. So she told him as best she could how it happened that she was there and what has been going on."

"She couldn't explain from across the room? She had to be in his arms to tell him this?"

"It got to be too much for her, and she was crying on his shoulder."

"Of course. It's such a broad and inviting shoulder." Sharley began to systematically shred the tissue.

Martin shrugged. "It wasn't any easier for her than this conversation is for me, Sharley."

She swallowed hard. He had a point. "Go on."

"Spence was shocked, and concerned."

"I can imagine."

"And he immediately saw the implications. If Charlotte came to hear of this . . ."

"It would be nasty, wouldn't it?"

"Very nasty indeed, I'm afraid. In the last year Charlotte's health has gotten to such a state ... Spence realized at a glance how stupid I'd been, and he was trying to find a way to minimize the fallout."

She remembered, now, what Spence had been telling Wendy as she walked in. *It can't go on like this,* he'd said. "Well, wasn't that cozy of him."

"If you're implying that Spence's motive was to protect me, you're wrong," Martin said sharply. "I believe his intention was to talk to me, to find some way to shock me back to my senses. But then you walked in. Naturally you were dismayed."

"That's the understatement of the year." Tears of fury burned her eyelids. "And he didn't bother to try to explain the truth!"

"Sharley, honey, think about it. He was still stunned himself, trying to think what to do, with no idea how I'd react if he confronted me with the facts, and the first thing you did was run straight to the house—straight to Charlotte."

Sharley was silent. He was right. Running to Charlotte had not been her intention, of course, but the effect had been the same.

"By the time Spence followed you, Charlotte was right there listening to every word."

Sharley remembered the shocked look on Spence's face when he realized Charlotte was in the room. She had thought at the time that he looked so stunned because Charlotte had begun to feel faint. But now that she thought about it, she realized Martin was right; that was the very instant Spence had stopped asking her to listen to him and asked for blind trust, instead.

But Martin had been there, too, she remembered. And he had done nothing. He had stood there and listened to her rip Spence to pieces, and he hadn't even tried to intervene.

Fury licked at her veins. "And you let me believe Spence was guilty. Uncle Martin, how could you?"

Martin said softly, "I'm not trying to defend myself, Sharley. I've already told you I'm a coward, but I assure you I wouldn't have stood by if I'd realized what had happened. Don't forget that I had no idea right then what was going on. I just knew that I'd walked into the middle of a fight. I wasn't even listening to you. All I could think of was Charlotte."

Sharley nodded a little. Just because the hurtful words she had thrown at Spence were engraved on her own heart didn't mean everyone else in the room had been hanging on each syllable.

"As soon as I found out what had happened—that it had been Wendy in the cottage—I wanted to tell you that it wasn't Spence's fault. But by then, you'd already shown him the door. You'd given his ring back and told him you never wanted to see him again."

"So you didn't bother trying to straighten things out?"

Martin's eyes were full of sadness. "It wasn't that way at all, Sharley. As soon as I could, I tried to reason with Spence. I told him that I wanted to explain—that I needed to explain! But he insisted I not tell you anything."

Sharley shook her head in confusion. "How could he forbid you to talk to me?"

"'Forbid' is a strong word. But he made it clear that it wouldn't do any good if I meddled, that I'd just stir things up worse, and he asked me to let it drop."

"Yes," she said almost to herself. "I've heard that tune before."

"And I was weak enough to accept that, Sharley. Not entirely to save my own skin," Martin added hastily, "but because I felt sure if the two of you just had a chance to cool off you'd work it out. But last week when I almost lost you…" He drew himself up very straight. "I can't hide behind Spence anymore and let him protect me at such a cost to himself."

Sharley nibbled at her thumbnail. "So, now that I know, what if I go straight to Charlotte right now and tell her?"

Martin said slowly, "You must do what you believe is right."

"But you don't think I will, do you? Do you expect me to become part of your conspiracy of silence, Uncle Martin?"

"I don't want to tell her, Sharley. I'm afraid of what the shock would do to her. And what would it accomplish? The affair is over. It's not going to happen again. And I am trying very hard to recapture my appreciation for the good things about my wife—the fine qualities, which are still there. I had let myself belittle those things because of my guilt, but maybe we can build on them, instead." He took a deep breath. "If you feel she must know, Sharley, I hope you'll give me just a little time. If someone must break it to her, please let it be me."

Sharley stood up. "I'm going to talk to Spence."

"I'm glad," Martin said simply. "He's quite a guy, your Spence."

She didn't turn around. "He's not my Spence, Uncle Martin."

"But you understand, don't you? He's completely innocent."

"Yes, I understand."

Martin sighed in relief. "Then it will be all right."

She didn't disillusion him. But as she walked to her car, she thought how ironic it was that the thing she had wanted so badly, had hoped and almost prayed for—the proof of

Spence's innocence—was no longer important at all. It simply didn't matter anymore.

The real issue was that their relationship hadn't been important enough to him to try to tell her the truth.

She wasn't surprised to find a new secretary—a gray-haired, motherly sort—installed in the administrative wing of Hudson Products. She wasn't even particularly startled when the woman said with a smile, "Hello, Miss Collins. I'll let Mr. Greenfield know you're here."

Uncle Martin at work, she thought. He'd probably called to warn Spence she was coming.

"I'll announce myself," Sharley said. But she stood for an instant with her hand on the doorknob, willing herself to turn it, before she could actually face him.

Spence looked up from the contract spread across his desk blotter, put down his fountain pen and stood up. "Come in, Sharley. So Martin finally worked up the nerve to unburden himself, did he?" His voice held a combative note, and there was no glint of humor in his eyes.

"How dare you try to keep him from telling me in the beginning!"

He moved around the desk and settled against the corner of it, arms folded across his chest. "What would you have done, Sharley?"

"What did you expect? That I'd run straight to Charlotte and tattle, with never a thought of what might happen to her?"

"You were so angry I had no idea what you'd do."

"I'm not a child to be pampered and sheltered!"

"If the whole thing blew up," Spence said slowly, "I didn't want you to be caught in the middle of the explosion."

"Oh? Well, thank you for protecting me from the guilt feelings if Charlotte died of the shock! You know, I'm amazed you didn't tell her straight out yourself, Spence. You seem so certain her health problems are all a fraud. Why would you hesitate to sock her with the truth?''

"I never said she's a fraud. I simply think she's stronger than she lets on. And whatever her health problems, there was no reason for anyone else to have to be involved. I thought it would be infinitely better for Martin to confess, instead of be caught. There would have been some hope of patching things up calmly then, without hysterics and heart palpitations, if he could tell her he'd made a mistake but had come to his senses in time and was making amends."

Sharley couldn't see her aunt taking such news calmly under any circumstances, but she had to admit Spence had a point. It was a bad situation no matter what, but some approaches were better than others.

"But you didn't let that happen, Sharley. You wouldn't listen, wouldn't give me time to talk to him. Before there was an opportunity to get anything straightened out, you'd made sure that Charlotte knew every nasty detail."

"I didn't!"

"What did you think you were doing, shouting at me in the hallway?"

She bit her lip.

"After that, for Martin to have told her he was the guilty one, not me, would have been like a confession wrenched out under torture. Admitting fault *after* you've been caught red-handed isn't the same thing at all."

Sharley said stubbornly, "You could have told me what was going on."

"In the hallway of Charlotte's house, with her standing there giving you instructions in etiquette? How could I have explained anything?"

She sat down on the arm of a chair. He was right. She had dealt him an impossible hand. Still . . .

"And when did Martin have the chance?" Spence went on. "When did he have an opportunity to talk to you without Charlotte right there in the room?"

Sharley was silent, trying to remember. She had actively avoided Martin those first few days, thinking he was naively trying to maneuver her and Spence into a reconciliation she found impossible to imagine. "Martin doesn't seem inclined to tell Aunt Charlotte the truth even now."

Spence sighed. "He may have a point. No matter how he explained it now, he wouldn't be able to eliminate the suspicion that he only confessed because he had no other choice—and even at that he'd perhaps fudge around the edges."

"And only tell as much of the truth as he has to to get by? Is that what you mean?"

"Exactly. Sometimes the truth causes hurt with no redeeming value. It might be better if Martin just cleaned up his act without Charlotte ever knowing about the affair."

Sharley frowned. "I'm not sure I understand what you mean."

"Sometimes the best way to apologize isn't to confess and say, 'I'm sorry'—it's to make sure whatever caused the hurt doesn't happen again. The affair is over—what good would it do now for Charlotte to know what happened? But that's for Martin to decide, not you and me."

"And by keeping quiet, he can avoid all the nasty consequences, can't he? I don't think you're as worried about Charlotte's feelings as you are about making sure Martin doesn't suffer any hurt from his own stupidity!"

"Maybe you're right," Spence mused. "I don't think you understand quite how nasty it would be if Charlotte took a notion to punish him."

Sharley shrugged. "I can't quite see her divorcing him. So what else could she do?"

"You really don't understand? Well, as long as we're clearing the decks... Sharley, do you even know how Hudson Products came into being?"

She was startled. What did Martin's business have to do with this?

Spence's voice was deliberate. "It was based on Charlotte's money."

She gasped. *"Charlotte's?* But that's impossible! If Charlotte had money, my mother would have had something, too. They were sisters."

"That seems reasonable, yes, if it had been family money. But it wasn't. Charlotte inherited it from her first husband."

Sharley said woodenly, "I never knew that."

There was a glint in Spence's eyes that might have been sympathy. "Martin worked for him as a machine operator—not much more than day labor. If it wasn't for Charlotte, that's what he'd still be. But Martin married his boss's widow, and she funded his business enterprise."

When a woman provides the money in a marriage, she has the right to call the shots.... That hadn't been just an observation, Sharley thought. When Charlotte said that, she had been stating a personal creed!

"From what I've picked up, it happened so long ago that I wouldn't be surprised if you never even heard that Charlotte was married before."

"I knew it. I guess I never thought about it." Sharley took a deep breath. "No wonder you were afraid I'd tell her. If she threw Martin out, where would you be? Right with him, no doubt."

His mouth tightened. "She couldn't actually do that. He owns the business. But in a divorce court, if she made an issue of her contribution to his success . . ."

Sharley went on recklessly, "No wonder you didn't want me caught in the middle! By the time the flak died down, I might have been disinherited!"

Spence walked around his desk and sat down. "Your inheritance or lack of it has never been an issue with me. But this whole conversation confirms that I was right in the beginning, doesn't it?"

"About what?"

"That it wouldn't pay to trouble you with explanations. And that I shouldn't waste my time begging you to understand."

"Because there wasn't anything to forgive?"

He looked at her for a long-drawn-out moment, and then said deliberately, "No, Sharley. Because there wasn't anything worth saving."

The words struck cruelly deep into her heart, and she struck back. "You never gave it a chance, Spence. You asked me to trust you, blindly, with no reason—nothing but your word. But you didn't trust me—not even enough to share the facts and believe I would use the truth responsibly!"

He pushed back his chair and crossed to the window. "Is this a demonstration of your responsible use of the truth? I didn't have to tell you about Charlotte's money, you know, and now you're using it against me."

Sharley bit her lip. He was right, and she was ashamed of herself. "I'm sorry. That was . . . insensitive of me. But you must agree that the circumstances were black, Spence. And you weren't willing to give any explanation at all—of course I had to conclude you didn't have one! Even at the cabin, with no one else around, you had all the time in the world to explain, and you wouldn't!''

''By then, it didn't matter anymore.'' His words had a deep ring of truth, and sadness.

Sharley whispered, ''What do you mean?''

''You'd told me all I needed to know that afternoon, shouting at me in the front hall. You wouldn't even try to take my word.'' He turned away from her to look out the window. ''A woman who doesn't trust me isn't the kind of woman I could love.''

Each word seemed to burn a hole into her heart. A final death knell to any hope she had ever had of working things out. Sharley swallowed hard and said quietly, ''I'm very sorry. You see, I loved you, Spence.''

He didn't even turn his head. ''Are you certain you didn't just love the idea of being in love?''

But it wasn't a question, really. He sounded as if he was stating a fact.

Sharley wet her lips. ''And I still love you,'' she whispered.

He didn't answer that at all.

Before she could humiliate herself further by bursting into tears, she turned on her heel and walked away, for the last time, from the man she loved.

CHAPTER TEN

THE CALENDAR SAID it was spring, and Sharley had noticed just that morning as she left the Hudson house to go to school that Martin's daffodils were beginning to bloom. Yesterday she'd even seen a fat robin hopping across the lawn. But now it was snowing—huge, fluffy, lazy flakes that probably wouldn't accumulate but made springtime seem only a distant dream.

She stood by the window in her classroom and looked out at the bird feeder, where a couple of goldfinches were scolding each other, to the playground beyond. The noise of children playing came softly to her ears, and she sighed and turned back to her desk. She had precious few minutes of quiet time to work, and she was wasting it.

The truth was she wasn't quite in top form yet. It was her first day back at school, and she was grateful there was only another hour to go. Perhaps the doctor, and Aunt Charlotte, hadn't been wrong....

She took the top paper off a stack of vocabulary tests and reached for a red pencil just as the classroom door opened. Amy Howell put her head around the corner and, seeing that Sharley was alone, came in.

"Are you sure you're doing all right?" she asked. "You look a little pale."

Sharley nodded. "I'm holding out."

Amy pulled a chair around and sank into it. "I bet you wish you'd gone skiing with us, after all."

Sharley smiled wryly. "Now that you mention it, yes. A twisted knee would have been nothing!" She reached into the bottom drawer of her desk and took out a small flat box. It had been sealed, then wrapped in a plastic bag that was stapled shut. She pushed the package across the desk.

Amy eyed it cautiously. "What's this?"

"You can't guess? It's only proper to return bridal gifts if one isn't going to be a bride."

"Oh, the negligee? What do you think I'm going to do with it? It was bad enough going into the store to buy it. Taking it back is out of the question." But—mercifully, Sharley thought—Amy slid the box under her arm and didn't pursue the matter further. "You brought your car today, didn't you?"

Sharley nodded. "I figured I wouldn't be eager for a walk home by the time the day was over. Why?"

"I have a big favor to ask. My car is in the shop having new tires put on. Can you drop me off downtown so I can pick it up? Or are you headed straight home to bed?"

"I'll take you. I have to stop at the dry cleaner's, anyway." She glanced at the window and sighed. "It looks as if I took my winter coats in too early."

The end-of-recess bell rang sharply, and a couple of minutes later kids started drifting back into the classroom. Some of them were wearing only light jackets, and most still had snowflakes caught in their hair.

"Great," Amy muttered. "I suppose we'll have them all sneezing for the rest of the week."

Sharley taught a short math lesson, then sat down and gratefully allowed one of her students to pass out work sheets to the class. She wondered how long it would take to get her stamina back.

She opened a desk drawer to pull out a textbook; at least she could work on next week's lesson plans for a few minutes. Under the book, at the bottom of the drawer, was the picture frame that used to sit on the corner of her desk—the snapshot of Spence and Wendy in the office at Hudson Products in happier days. Sharley stared at it for a full minute, and then she turned the frame facedown. She couldn't quite bring herself to destroy the picture, for that would be saying a final goodbye, and she was not yet strong enough to do so. It was over; she knew that. But surely there was no sin in continuing to wish for a little while that things could be different....

When she looked up, sensing a new presence in the classroom, she actually thought for a moment she was seeing things. Just inside the door stood Wendy Taylor, looking around hesitantly.

Sharley pushed back her chair and crossed the room. "May I help you?" she said softly.

"I'd like to talk to you. But I'll wait till your class is over."

"I have a minute now." She ushered Wendy into the hall and left the classroom door ajar—open enough to hear any budding revolution inside, but not enough that the children could overhear a quiet conversation.

"I'm sorry to come here," Wendy said. "But it was the only place I knew I could talk to you alone. I owe you an apology."

There must be a hundred things for Wendy to apologize for, Sharley thought, and wondered which one was bothering Wendy's conscience. "Why?" she asked bluntly.

"For begging Spence not to tell you what was going on."

Sharley's eyebrows raised.

"You were so angry that I was scared—terrified of what you'd do. Now I believe I underestimated you."

"Because Martin confessed to me and I haven't betrayed his confidence?"

"That, and other things. I'm sorry, Sharley. If I'd let Spence explain right then, before you left the cottage..."

That's right, Wendy, Sharley wanted to say. You'd have done us all a favor if you just hadn't interfered. But that wasn't quite the truth, and she knew it wasn't fair to put all the blame on Wendy. "No one has that much power over Spence. If he'd really wanted to tell me, he would have."

Wendy frowned a little. "Not after you'd questioned whether he was telling the truth. His word is a big thing with him, Sharley."

The comment stung. Sharley wanted to say, *A little late for this chat, don't you think?* But instead, she said, "I need to get back to my students, Wendy. Is there anything else I can do for you?"

Wendy's face paled a little. "I just wanted you to know that I'm going away. Martin isn't sending me and I'm not running, but we agreed it would be best if I didn't stay in Hammond's Point." Her voice was full of pain. "You don't need to be afraid of anything blowing up in your face again. I care for Martin too much to do that. And I respect the decision he's made."

Sharley's throat tightened. The woman really does love him, she thought, and she's as miserable as any of us. She put a hand out to take Wendy's. "I'm sorry things couldn't have been easier."

"For both of us," Wendy agreed. She squeezed Sharley's fingers for a moment, then she turned and hurried down the long hall to the outside doors.

The streets were lightly frosted with snow by the time the school day ended, and slick spots lay where they were least expected. The droves of children walking home, heedless of the difficulties faced by drivers, meant that all of Sharley's concentration had to be focused on the road.

As they stopped for a school-crossing light, Amy said cautiously, "I saw you had a visitor this afternoon."

Sharley answered only with a quizzical look.

"Do you mean you're on such chummy terms with Wendy Taylor all of a sudden that you forgot she came by?"

"Not exactly," Sharley said uneasily. Amy's question was a difficult one; if Sharley admitted that she no longer held Wendy in contempt, it was bound to lead to questions. Yet she could hardly keep up a facade of hatred, either, when she honestly felt sympathy for the woman.

Sharley was beginning to appreciate the impossible position Spence had found himself in. Once the reasons for their broken engagement had become public knowledge, any attempt at an alternative explanation of why Spence and Wendy had been together in the gardener's cottage would have thrown suspicion wildly on anyone within a mile of the main participants. No wonder Spence had felt his only option was to take the heat.

She stopped outside the tire place, and Amy gathered up her books from the floor. But she didn't get out of the car. She looked thoughtfully at Sharley and said, "There's one more thing you probably ought to know. I wrote it off as catty rumor, and I'm sure that's all it is, but it doesn't seem to be dying down."

Sharley sighed. "What now?"

"The talk around town is that Spence did it on purpose."

"Had this alleged affair with Wendy, you mean?"

"What do you mean 'alleged'? Never mind. It's not the affair that's being talked about—it's the carbon monoxide."

Sharley's eyes widened in astonishment.

"The newest story around town is that he followed you up to the cabin to get you to reconsider the breakup, and—"

"That's ridiculous."

"And when you wouldn't, he tried to follow in his father's footsteps—and take you with him."

Sharley was stunned. The idea that Spence would consider suicide, much less murder, was outlandish. How terribly easy it was to twist the truth into a better story!

A driver behind her honked impatiently. Amy opened her door and said, "Sorry to be the one to tell you."

"No," Sharley said automatically. "Don't be. See you tomorrow." She put the car into gear; it skidded slightly on the snow, and automatically she pulled it back into line.

She almost drove past the dry cleaner's, remembering her errand only at the last moment. And it took effort to listen to the clerk's cheerful comments about the weather, and make an appropriate response.

She was fumbling in her wallet when the clerk added, "We found this in one of the pockets, Miss Collins." She held out an envelope.

"Thank you. I've gotten so careless...." Sharley handed over the money and reached for the envelope. It almost burned her fingers.

She had seen it before, but the memory seemed aeons old. Her hand began to tremble. She had fished that envelope out of the mailbox at the gardener's cottage, and stuffed it into her coat pocket, intending to read it once she was inside. But then her world had collapsed, and she had forgotten Spence's note. She had thrown the coat into the closet and had not worn it since.

She carefully hung the plastic-wrapped clothes in the back of her car, as if the fate of the universe was balanced on how conscientious she was just now. And she drove to the park, to the isolated corner where they'd had their quiet winter picnic, before she carefully slit the envelope and pulled out Spence's last note.

It was short, just a few lines, written on Hudson Products letterhead. She could almost see him, sitting at his desk with his fountain pen. And she could almost hear his voice. . . .

"Sharley, love— Only a week now till our wedding. Things are getting so hectic there isn't time to talk. Does that ever bother you—that there isn't time?"

"Yes," she whispered. "But we were going to have all the time in the world . . ." She had to blink away tears before she could continue reading.

"I want you to know that you've given me the most valuable gift anyone could, Sharley. Your love, of course, and even more important to me, your trust. You know what my father was, but you may not realize how few people in this town are able to take my word for anything—because they put their faith in him and he abused their trust. You've never doubted me. I think that was the first thing I loved about you. The first of many. I can't say all this straight out to you—it sounds too sentimental. But I wanted you to know."

Sharley leaned her forehead against the steering wheel.

He had slipped this letter into the mailbox and gone inside the cottage to work and to wait for Sharley. Instead, he had found Wendy.

"And then I walked in," Sharley said. "And his life came crashing down around his head."

She wished she could cry. But this pain was too deep, too severe to be relieved by tears.

What was it Wendy had said this afternoon? *His word is a big thing with him.* Even Wendy had understood what Sharley had not.

He must have assumed, if he'd taken time to think about it at all, that she had read this letter long ago—maybe even before she had walked into the cottage. No wonder he had reacted as he had; she must have sounded very heartless that day.

If only she had listened earlier. Not on that horrible day at the cottage—it was already too late then—but long before. If only she had tried to know him better, to understand what made him different, what made him the very special man she loved. Then she would have realized in time how crucial it was to Spence that she believe him.

The flames of their love were gone. There was no question about that; she had doused them herself. But at least, after reading his letter, she was confident—as she hadn't been since the day in the cottage—that he had loved her once.

Now the question was whether the ashes of that love were completely cold, or if there were one last warm ember somewhere—and a chance to fan the fire back to life.

AT DINNER, Sharley only picked at her food. She didn't even pretend to listen to the conversation; her thoughts were on her own troubles. She was going back over that last conversation with Spence, trying to find some scrap of encouragement to keep her going. It wasn't easy; honesty forced her to admit that she would probably be wasting her time if she tried to convince him that there was still hope for them. What was she to do, anyway? Tell him she was sorry for not understanding? It was a start, of course, but she didn't expect mere words to make much difference. No, there had to be a better way to make amends.

What was it he'd said about that? Sometimes the best way to apologize was to make sure the hurt doesn't happen again. Yes, that was it.

She pushed a piece of salmon around on her plate while she considered. That approach would take time and patience, and perhaps he might never see what she was trying to say. Still, she had nothing but time, and she might as well learn to practice patience.

Charlotte, watching her toy with her food, finally said, "Well, I hoped you've learned something about listening to your doctor, Sharley."

"What? Oh, I'm just tired. Tomorrow will be easier."

"Surely you're not going back till you're completely well!"

Martin intervened. "Sharley can make her own decisions, Charlotte."

Something was different about Martin, Sharley thought. There was a new note in his voice, but the change was more than that. It was as if he had regained his self-respect, and he wasn't afraid anymore.

"Very foolish," Charlotte muttered. "That's all I've got to say."

Martin waited until Libby had cleared the main course and brought in a white-chocolate cheesecake. "Maybe we should go away for a while, Charlotte. It would take your mind off things. Now that you're feeling better—"

"Who said I was feeling better?"

"You're certainly stronger than you were last fall," Martin said patiently. "But if you're not up to a strenuous trip, how about a cruise? That would let you rest and recuperate. Salt air for a couple of months—"

"A couple of months?"

"Yes. It would be just the thing. We could go around the world, perhaps. I'll look into it."

"*Months*?" Charlotte repeated. "You'd leave Spence in charge of Hudson Products for months?"

"Why not?" Martin said coolly. "He's been running the whole plant for a year now. I'm only a figurehead, Charlotte, and when I retire, Spence will take over." He took a bite of cheesecake and added in a muffled undertone, "If he's still here."

Sharley put down her fork. "What do you mean?"

Martin's gaze was warm and sympathetic. "Just what I said. *If* he's still here, and the way things are looking..."

His unfinished sentence just hung there, ominously. Of course Sharley didn't really need to hear more; it didn't take a genius to figure out what Martin meant. Spence had had enough, that was clear. He was going away. There would be no time, after all, to show him how much she regretted what had happened. Sharley wanted to scream, but even in the middle of her own pain, she understood. What was left for him in Hammond's Point? Even the reputation he'd tried so hard to rebuild was being chipped away, through no fault of his own.

"Aunt Charlotte," she said suddenly, "remember that reception you wanted me to attend in your place? It's tonight, isn't it? What time does it start?"

"It would be polite of you not to interrupt your elders," Charlotte pointed out. "It begins at eight. But if you're too tired even to eat your dinner, you certainly shouldn't be going out for the evening."

Sharley was already on her feet. "I won't be late."

Sharley had no doubt that with a famous musician as bait, the cream of Hammond's Point society would turn out for the reception. She was not disappointed. As she made her way through the crush, she ticked names off her mental list; yes, the gossips were out in force. It wouldn't take long for what she had to say to make the rounds of the town.

She took a glass of champagne from a waiter's tray, more for something to hold on to than because she wanted it. Her hands were trembling; now that the moment was here, she had no idea how to proceed.

She turned toward the tea table and ran headlong into Spence. She pulled back like a startled fawn; it would have been so much easier if she didn't have to face him, too, while she spoke her piece.

The champagne in her glass surged like a tidal wave, threatening to burst over the rim of the goblet and drench the front of his shirt. Spence's hand closed firmly on her wrist and held the glass at a safe distance.

His grip was just short of painful, and Sharley couldn't help wincing as she looked up at him.

"Sorry," he said shortly, and his hand dropped to his side.

"My fault. Of course soaking you with champagne wouldn't be the only thing you have to forgive me for," she said quietly.

Spence had already started to turn away, but he swung back to face her. He looked puzzled, she thought, perhaps even a bit confused.

A matron nearby sniffed. "I never thought I'd see the day," she murmured to a friend.

Spence nodded coldly at the woman and took a step away. Sharley's heart twisted. She had been taught from childhood to disregard that kind of rudeness; Spence, she thought, had learned the hard way to ignore it—or at least to pretend it didn't affect him.

Sharley wheeled around to face the matron. "Perhaps you're surprised that I'm the one who's apologizing?" She did not try to keep her voice low.

A murmur rippled through the crowd.

Spence was beside her again, a hand on her arm. His voice was low. "You've had too much champagne, Sharley."

"I haven't had so much as a sip." She looked up at him and smiled. "Don't worry, I'll be careful. But there are some things I have to say, Spence." She raised her voice a little, so that even though she was looking at Spence, it was clear she was talking to everyone.

"Breaking my engagement was the biggest mistake I have ever made in my life," she said clearly, "and I deeply regret my foolishness. My only excuse is that I did not truly appreciate the quality of the man I was engaged to marry until I saw him perform two of the most unselfish acts I have ever known."

Spence's face was pale, and his jaw was set. Sharley didn't know if it was shock or anger that made him look that way, or fear that she would tell the crowd about those two unselfish acts—that he had not only saved her life, but protected Martin. She told herself it didn't matter; it was too late to stop now.

"And I want him—and all of you—to know that if I had it in my power to make a different choice, I would do it. I would be honored to be his wife."

Five endless seconds ticked by, and Spence was silent. Sharley turned away toward the makeshift cloakroom. If she had humiliated herself, she thought, it was in a good cause. Now it was time for a fast exit, before the questions began to fly.

She saw the famous musician standing beside his hostess, and she paused. "I'm sorry to have trampled all over your party."

He bowed gallantly. Sharley didn't hear what he said.

She didn't quite know why she went directly to the gardener's cottage. She only knew that she wanted to be

alone, and no one would disturb her there. She didn't
bother to turn on the lights. The floodlights out in the
garden reflected off the patchy snow and bounced through
the windows, casting long intricate shadows; once her eyes
grew accustomed to the weird patterns, she could make her
way around the cottage with no problem at all.

She saw that the rest of the furniture had been delivered
and wondered when it had arrived. A pair of club chairs
stood by the fireplace now, and in the tiny dining nook was
an intimate table for two. The cottage smelled of fresh
paint and new leather. But those pleasant aromas were
mixed with an aura she could only call forlorn emptiness.
By now, this little house should have smelled of cookies
and coffee and spices of all kinds—and the aura should
have been one of love.

She stroked the back of the love seat, still awkwardly out
of place at the side of the living room, just as it had been
that day almost three weeks ago....

She plunged both hands into her coat pockets, and her
fingertips touched Spence's note. She pulled it out and held
it between her palms. It was too dark to read in the cottage, but the feel of the paper crackling under her touch
was comforting. Once, he had loved her. Even tonight, she
could see in his eyes the memory of that love—but it was
only a memory.

She sank into one of the new club chairs and stared at
the empty fireplace, caressing the note as if it were written
in braille and her fingertips could recognize the words. She
had done all she could, she reminded herself. Perhaps at
least he would come to see her before he left Hammond's
Point....

She was thinking about that when she looked up, and for
a moment she actually wondered if she had conjured up
the tall shadow leaning against the back of the love seat.

Then he moved closer, and his step was so silent he might have been a ghost.

He didn't speak, and the silence dragged out for what seemed forever. Sharley's fingers were trembling; she knew because the crisp letterhead paper rustled a little. She looked down at it. "I was reading your note."

"You'll ruin your eyes." He moved toward the doorway and the switches that controlled the lights.

"I only got it today," she said quietly.

He paused. "But you said—"

"I picked it up that afternoon, yes. In the shock, I forgot, and I didn't read it till today." She looked down at the white blur in her lap. "Did you mean this, Spence?"

He stood as still as a statue, and the darkness in the room seemed to intensify.

Sharley said, "I'm sorry. Of course you meant it then, or you wouldn't have said it. And now, well, I guess I already know the answer to that, don't I?"

"Do you, Sharley?" His voice was quiet. "That was a very... gracious thing you did tonight."

Gracious. He could have called it many things, but that particular word stung her pride somehow. It minimized the effort, the effect, the importance of what she'd tried to do. He made it sound as if she had done no more than any ordinary hostess would to put a guest at ease.

"I owed you one," she said stiffly.

"Is that why you did it?"

She didn't answer directly. "At least they'll stop accusing you of trying to murder me."

"You can't have taken that seriously. I didn't."

"Oh, you didn't?" Sharley snapped. "Then why is Martin so sure you're leaving Hammond's Point over it?"

He didn't answer for a moment, and when he spoke his voice was deep and dry. "Martin knows perfectly well why I'm thinking of leaving Hammond's Point."

Then it was true. Her fingertips dug into the soft upholstery of the club chair. "Take me with you, Spence!" The words were out, in a mournful wail, before she realized it. She saw the shock in his eyes and plunged on before she could think better of it or consider how embarrassed she would be in the end. She jumped up. "I don't expect you to marry me. I just don't want to be shut out of your life. Give me another chance, Spence!" She was beside him by then, hands clutching the lapels of his coat.

He flipped a switch, and the lamps came on.

Sharley blinked in the sudden glare. The light made her feel naked, and foolish. She didn't let go of his lapels, but she couldn't look at him. She fixed her gaze on a solid gray stripe in his tie, instead.

"You'd go with me?" he said quietly.

She nodded.

"No job. No plans. No destination."

"That doesn't matter. I don't know what you'll do any more than you do, but I believe in you. I made the mistake of not trusting you once, Spence. I won't do it again." She took a deep breath. "I came to your hospital room that day to tell you that I believed you, that I would take your word for it, before I ever knew what really happened. I don't expect you to accept that, but it's true."

Slowly his arms closed around her. Sharley felt as if she was being wrapped in a very large, very comforting blanket, one that would never let her feel the cold again. She gave a tiny sob and buried her face in his shoulder, clinging to him as if he was the only solid pillar in a very uncertain world.

"I should have told you," he whispered. "I expected too much, asking for blind trust when you'd caught me in such a compromising position. But when you looked at me like that and said that you didn't love me enough to take my word for it..."

"I didn't realize," she managed to say. "I hadn't considered that you could feel inadequate, Spence. It never occurred to me to wonder if you had doubts about yourself."

"You cut me to the heart when you said that. I'd never lied to you, Sharley, and I never intended to."

"So you wouldn't tell me anything at all."

He nodded. "I guess I didn't realize then that not sharing things was lying of a different sort."

"What kind of things?"

"Like how scared I was, even before Wendy messed things up."

"Scared?" she whispered.

He sighed. "Because I loved you so deeply."

She remembered what he'd said in his office that day when she told him she loved him. "And you were afraid I didn't love you as much as I loved the idea of being in love." She put her forehead against his shoulder. "You might have been right, a little. I know I didn't really appreciate you till I'd lost you."

"When you turned your back on me that day, something shattered, Sharley."

"And that's when you felt there was nothing between us worth saving?"

He nodded, his chin brushing softly against her hair. "And still I loved you. No matter how much I wanted to wipe that out of my mind, I couldn't."

She knew exactly how that felt.

"I went up to the cabin to exorcise you—and you were there. Do you have any idea how difficult it was for me to be around you under those conditions? Every time I turned around you were practically in my arms, begging to be kissed—"

"I was not!" she said indignantly, and turned a little pink at the skeptical look he gave her. "Not much, anyway."

"Sometimes it wasn't quite so obvious. The morning you sat beside the fire and dried your hair was the most sensual display I've ever seen. Spun gold, shimmering in the firelight, and you didn't even know how beautiful you were." He let his fingers slide through her hair.

Sharley looked up at him through her lashes. "If that's the way it affected you, maybe I should work out some variations."

He laughed, and kissed her. Sharley relaxed against him, feeling as if she could melt straight into his body. The bone-deep ache that had grown to be a part of her was draining slowly away.

"Don't worry about rehearsing," Spence said finally. "You don't need practice—you even wake up sexy. You rub your eyes like a baby..." He sobered abruptly. "Of course, that night when you didn't want to wake up—"

"Don't," she said. "It's over, and we were lucky."

He nodded, and the haunted look died from his eyes.

"Perhaps we'll be stronger because of everything that's happened," Sharley whispered. "I know I needed a chance to grow up a little, to appreciate what I had."

"Maybe we both did," Spence said quietly. "Even after you told me you still loved me, I was afraid to hope that we could salvage something. Too afraid to take the chance. When you made your grandstand play tonight to save me from the gossip, I couldn't decide whether to kiss you or hit my head against the nearest wall I was so angry with myself. How could I blame you for not trusting me when *I* hadn't trusted *you?*"

Sharley smiled and let her fingertips wander through his hair. "Your poor head. Or should I say, poor wall? It might not have been as hard as your head is."

"I didn't do it. I thought there had already been quite enough of a scene."

"Well," Sharley said reasonably, "if it accomplished the purpose..."

"It was worth it, all right. Still, do you have any idea what Charlotte is going to say to you when she hears what you did?"

Sharley gave a tiny gurgle of laughter. "Yes. Not that I'm going to let it bother me. Where are we going, Spence? I mean, you must have a direction in mind, at least, and I'd like to know what sort of clothes to pack."

"How about right here? Hammond's Point?"

She pulled back a little. "What?"

He gathered her even more closely into his arms. "I've been thinking of leaving, yes. Not because of the gossip— I've stood a whole lot worse than that—but because I didn't think I could take living here and seeing you and loving you, and not having you."

"Did Martin know that?" she said suspiciously.

"Yes. I had to tell him, you see—"

"The little schemer!"

"Because he offered me a chance to buy Hudson Products."

Her eyes widened in astonishment.

"He realized how uncomfortable it was going to be trying to put things back as they once were. And he thought it was time I had a chance to prove what I could do." He held her a little away from him. "It's neither a gift nor a bribe, Sharley, just a fair deal—and it isn't going to be easy to swing it. We may be facing some lean times."

"We?" she asked demurely.

"How about it, Sharley? Shall we try again?"

She looked down at the gray stripe in his tie again and said soberly, "I didn't pull that stunt tonight to maneuver you into proposing, Spence."

"I know. The question stands."

"And I never let you properly propose to me the first time, either. I had nightmares about that, afterward, wondering if you'd ever really wanted to marry me at all."

He kissed her long and thoroughly, and when she was breathless and clinging to him, he put his cheek down against her hair and said, "It's probably just as well. I might never have actually gotten around to asking."

"What?" The word was almost a shriek.

He cupped her face in his hands. "As long as I didn't ask, you couldn't refuse, so I could keep on dreaming."

"Oh," Sharley said softly. "In that case..." She stopped.

Spence sighed. "I suppose this means you want a proposal in form? All right, have your pound of flesh." He dropped to one knee and clasped her hand to his heart. "Sharley, will you marry me?"

She looked down at him thoughtfully, straightened his tie and ran her free hand over the soft lapels of his jacket till her fingers rested comfortably at the back of his neck. "I'll have to think about it," she murmured. "This is all so sudden."

For an instant, he stared at her as if she had suddenly sprouted an extra nose. Then he grinned and gave a quick tug to her hand, pulling her down onto the carpet and pinning her there with his body.

"Sudden, nothing," he said. "You're two weeks late for the wedding as it is. We've had a honeymoon to forget, my love. What about having one to remember?"

His kiss was deep and long and satisfying, and it left Sharley too luxuriously dizzy to do anything but nod.

Let

HARLEQUIN ROMANCE®
take you

BACK TO THE

Come to the Tully T Ranch near Fortune, Texas (a blink-and-you'll-miss-it cow town!).

Meet Evelina Pettit, better known as Evvie, a schoolteacher from Houston who comes to help with the "Return to Good Fortune" celebrations. *And meet* rancher Ryan Garrison. He wants a wife—even though he doesn't believe in love. *Read* Virginia Hart's THE PERFECT SCOUNDREL and watch what happens when the schoolmarm meets the cowboy!

THE PERFECT SCOUNDREL is our next Back to the Ranch title, available in March, wherever Harlequin Books are sold.

RANCH10

Relive the romance...
Harlequin and Silhouette
are proud to present

 *by Request* ™

A program of collections of three complete novels by the most-requested
authors with the most-requested themes. Be sure to look for one volume each
month with three complete novels by top-name authors.

In September: **BAD BOYS**
Dixie Browning
Ann Major
Ginna Gray

No heart is safe when these hot-blooded hunks are in town!

In October: **DREAMSCAPE**
Jayne Ann Krentz
Anne Stuart
Bobby Hutchinson

Something's happening! But is it love or magic?

In December: **SOLUTION: MARRIAGE** Debbie Macomber
Annette Broadrick
Heather Graham Pozzessere

Marriages in name only have a way of leading to love....

Available at your favorite retail outlet.

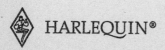 HARLEQUIN®   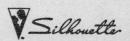 *Silhouette*

My Valentine
1994

Celebrate the most romantic day of the year with
MY VALENTINE 1994
a collection of original stories, written by
four of Harlequin's most popular authors...

MARGOT DALTON
MURIEL JENSEN
MARISA CARROLL
KAREN YOUNG

Available in February, wherever
Harlequin Books are sold.

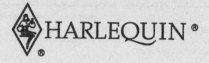
HARLEQUIN ®

VAL94

**Fifty red-blooded, white-hot, true-blue hunks
from every State in the Union!**

Look for MEN MADE IN AMERICA! Written by some
of our most poplar authors, these stories feature fifty of
the strongest, sexiest men, each from a different state in
the union!

Two titles available every other month at your favorite
retail outlet.

In March, look for:

TANGLED LIES by Anne Stuart (Hawaii)
ROGUE'S VALLEY by Kathleen Creighton (Idaho)

In May, look for:

LOVE BY PROXY by Diana Palmer (Illinois)
POSSIBLES by Lass Small (Indiana)

You won't be able to resist MEN MADE IN AMERICA!

Relive the romance...
Harlequin and Silhouette
are proud to present

A program of collections of three complete novels by the most requested
authors with the most requested themes. Be sure to look for one volume each
month with three complete novels by top name authors.

In January: **WESTERN LOVING**   Susan Fox
                                   JoAnn Ross
                                   Barbara Kaye

Loving a cowboy is easy—taming him isn't!

In February: **LOVER, COME BACK!**   Diana Palmer
                                       Lisa Jackson
                                       Patricia Gardner Evans

It was over so long ago—yet now they're calling, "Lover, Come Back!"

In March: **TEMPERATURE RISING**   JoAnn Ross
                                     Tess Gerritsen
                                     Jacqueline Diamond

Falling in love—just what the doctor ordered!

Available at your favorite retail outlet.

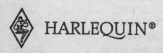 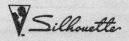

HARLEQUIN®   Silhouette

HARLEQUIN®

Don't miss these Harlequin favorites by some of our most distinguished authors!
And now, you can receive a discount by ordering two or more titles!

HT#25409	THE NIGHT IN SHINING ARMOR by JoAnn Ross	$2.99	☐
HT#25471	LOVESTORM by JoAnn Ross	$2.99	☐
HP#11463	THE WEDDING by Emma Darcy	$2.89	☐
HP#11592	THE LAST GRAND PASSION by Emma Darcy	$2.99	☐
HR#03188	DOUBLY DELICIOUS by Emma Goldrick	$2.89	☐
HR#03248	SAFE IN MY HEART by Leigh Michaels	$2.89	☐
HS#70464	CHILDREN OF THE HEART by Sally Garrett	$3.25	☐
HS#70524	STRING OF MIRACLES by Sally Garrett	$3.39	☐
HS#70500	THE SILENCE OF MIDNIGHT by Karen Young	$3.39	☐
HI#22178	SCHOOL FOR SPIES by Vickie York	$2.79	☐
HI#22212	DANGEROUS VINTAGE by Laura Pender	$2.89	☐
HI#22219	TORCH JOB by Patricia Rosemoor	$2.89	☐
HAR#16459	MACKENZIE'S BABY by Anne McAllister	$3.39	☐
HAR#16466	A COWBOY FOR CHRISTMAS by Anne McAllister	$3.39	☐
HAR#16462	THE PIRATE AND HIS LADY by Margaret St. George	$3.39	☐
HAR#16477	THE LAST REAL MAN by Rebecca Flanders	$3.39	☐
HH#28704	A CORNER OF HEAVEN by Theresa Michaels	$3.99	☐
HH#28707	LIGHT ON THE MOUNTAIN by Maura Seger	$3.99	☐

Harlequin Promotional Titles

#83247	YESTERDAY COMES TOMORROW by Rebecca Flanders	$4.99	☐
#83257	MY VALENTINE 1993	$4.99	☐
	(short-story collection featuring Anne Stuart, Judith Arnold, Anne McAllister, Linda Randall Wisdom)		

(limited quantities available on certain titles)

	AMOUNT	$
DEDUCT:	10% DISCOUNT FOR 2+ BOOKS	$
ADD:	POSTAGE & HANDLING	$
	($1.00 for one book, 50¢ for each additional)	
	APPLICABLE TAXES*	$ _____
	TOTAL PAYABLE	$ _____
	(check or money order—please do not send cash)	

To order, complete this form and send it, along with a check or money order for the total above, payable to Harlequin Books, to: **In the U.S.:** 3010 Walden Avenue, P.O. Box 9047, Buffalo, NY 14269-9047; **In Canada:** P.O. Box 613, Fort Erie, Ontario, L2A 5X3.

Name: _____

Address: _____ City: _____

State/Prov.: _____ Zip/Postal Code: _____

*New York residents remit applicable sales taxes.
 Canadian residents remit applicable GST and provincial taxes.

HBACK-JM